Silvia Mann

THE MODERN LIBRARY
OF THE WORLD'S BEST BOOKS

A DREAMER'S TALES AND OTHER STORIES

Turn to the end of this volume
for a complete list of titles
in the Modern Library

A DREAMER'S TALES
AND OTHER STORIES

By LORD DUNSANY

INTRODUCTION BY PADRIAC COLUM

THE MODERN LIBRARY

PUBLISHERS :: :: NEW YORK

Manufactured in the United States of America
Bound for THE MODERN LIBRARY *by* H. Wolff

CONTENTS

BObthomtc

INTRODUCTION

A tall and spare young man wearing incongruous spectacles across most eager eyes was addressing an audience in a literary society in Dublin. Somebody said "He looks like a portrait of Robert Louis Stevenson," and indeed in the sparse moustache, in the eager eyes and in the suggestion of hollowness in the face, there was a resemblance. He was speaking on poetry and by his intense interest in his subject he was able to enliven his audience as though by the spell of poetry itself. Every poem he quoted seemed inspired. He had none of the tricks, but everybody could see he was a natural orator.

He was Lord Dunsany whose plays "The Glittering Gate," and "King Argimines and the Unknown Warrior" had been produced by the Irish Theatre (in 1909 and 1911). He was an officer in the British Army, a notable cricketeer and a good huntsman and had already been through one war. But one could see that what he prized above all were the things of the imagination.

He was praising the work of a young poet who belonged to his own territory in Ireland—the County Meath. He spoke of that county with such gusto that one felt that Dunsany himself would put the fact that he was a Meath man before the fact that he was an Irishman. Meath is Ireland's middle county. It has the richest soil, and for that reason it has been fought for by every conquistidore who broke into Ireland. Before the Normans came Meath had already a thousand years of story. It was the demesne of the Ard-ri, the Imperator of the Celtic-Irish states. In Meath is Tara which was so sacred and venerable that the

King who obtained possession of it had the other Kings of
ancient Ireland for his vassals. And Cuchullain whose name
evokes a whole cycle of myth and story had part of Meath
for his patrimony. "Even the man who beat Napoleon was
a Meath man," Lord Dunsany exclaimed. That is not true,
however. Wellington, though he came of a Meath family,
happened to be born in another Irish county.

Lord Dunsany's progenitors, the Norman-Irish or Norse-
Irish Plunketts, were able to root themselves in this famous,
not to say fabled, Irish territory. The first conquistidore
founded two lordships—the lordship of Fingall and the lordship of Dunsany. The domains, the castles and the titles
remain from the thirteenth century and form the oldest
baronial possessions in the British Islands. Lord Dunsany
then belongs to one of the half dozen families in the British
peerage who are of actual Norman descent.

His father it is of interest to note was a considerable
orator, and his uncle is the well-known Irish statesman, Sir
Horace Plunkett. Edward John Moreton Drax Plunkett, the
present Lord Dunsany, went to an English public school and
an English university; he became an officer in the Guards,
and he had gone through the South African war before he
began to write.

His work began like an ancient literature with mythology.
He told us first about the gods of the lands where his kings,
his priests and his shepherds were to abide. The gods were
remote upon Pegana, but below them were the thousand
Home Gods—Roon, the god of Going, whose temples stand
beyond the farthest hills; Kilooloogung, the Lord of Arising
Smoke; Jabim, who sits behind the house to lament the
things that are broken and cast away; Triboogie, the Lord
of Dusk, whose children are the shadows; Pitsu, who strokes
the cat; Hobith, who calms the dog; Habinabah, who is
Lord of Glowing Embers; old Gribaun, who sits in the heart
of the fire and turns the wood to ash. "And when it is dark,
all in the hour of Triboogie," says the Chapter in "The Gods

of Pegana" that tells of the Thousand Home Gods, "Hish creepeth from the forest, the Lord of Silence, whose children are the bats who have broken the command of their father, but in a voice that is ever so low. Hish husheth the mouse and all the whispers in the night; he maketh all noises still. Only the cricket rebelleth. But Hish has sent against him such a spell that after he hath cried a thousand times his voice may be heard no more, but becometh part of the silence."

After he had written "The Gods of Pegana" Lord Dunsany discovered a figure that was more significant for him than any of his gods—the figure of Time. "Suddenly the swart figure of Time stood up before the gods, both hands dripping with blood and a red sword dangling idly from his fingers." Time had overthrown Sardathrion, the city they had built for their solace, and when the oldest of the gods questioned him "Time looked him in the face and edged towards him, fingering with his dripping fingers the hilt of his nimble sword." Over and over again he tells of the cities that were wonderful before Time prevailed against them—Sardathrion, with its onyx lion looming limb by limb from the dusk; Babbulkund, that was called by those who loved her "The City of Marvel," and by those who hated her "The City of the Dog," where over the roofs of her palace chambers "winged lions flit like bats, the size of every one is the size of the lions of God, and the wings are larger than any wing created"; Bethmoora, where window after window pours into the dusk its "lion-frightening light." We all must regret that these stories by Dunsany were not amongst the stories we read in our youth. "Had I read "The Fall of Babbulkund," or "Idle Days on the Yann" when I was a boy," says W. B. Yeats, "I had perhaps been changed for better or worse, and looked to that first reading as the creation of my world; for when we are young the less circumstantial, the further from common life a book is, the more does it touch our hearts and make us dream. We are

idle, unhappy, exorbitant, and like the young Blake admit
no city beautiful that is not paved with gold and silver."

From the making of tales he has gone on to the making
of plays, and he has brought into the theatre the impressive
simplicity of his myths and stories. His kings and beggars
and slaves are utterly simple and single-minded; they have
nothing but a passion or a vision or a faith. He came to the
theatre with little knowledge of what is called dramatic con-
struction, but with an astonishing feeling for dramatic situation. It is by virtue of this feeling for situation that his
"Gods of the Mountain," his "King Argimines and the
Unknown Warrior," and his "Night at an Inn," are such
effective theatrical pieces.

As fundamental as the sense of situation should be the
dramatist's sense of exalted speech. There are words, words,
words, but no speech, let alone the exaltation of it in the
theatre of to-day. Lord Dunsany, with W. B. Yeats and
J. M. Synge has restored speech to the theatre and has made
it exalted. "O warrior spirit," cries King Argimines, apos-
trophising the dead man whose sword he has found in the
slave-fields—"O warrior spirit, wherever thou wanderest,
whoever be thy gods; whether they punish thee or whether
they bless thee; O kingly spirit that once laid here this
sword, behold I pray to thee having no gods to pray to, for
the god of my nation was broken in three by night. Mine
arm is stiff with three years' slavery and remembers not the
sword. But guide thy sword till I have slain six men and
armed the strongest slaves, and thou shalt have sacrifice
every year of a hundred goodly oxen. And I shall build in
Ithara a temple to thy memory wherein all that enter in
shall remember thee, so shalt thou be honored and envied
among the dead, for the dead are very jealous of remembrance. Aye, though thou wert a robber that took men's
lives unrighteously, yet shall rare spices smoulder in thy
temple and little maidens sing and new-plucked flowers deck
the solemn aisles . . . O but it has a good blade this old

green sword; thou wouldst not like to see it miss its mark, thou wouldst not like to see it go thirsting into the air; so huge a sword should have its marrowy bone. Come into my right arm, O ancient spirit, O unknown warrior's soul. And if thou hast the ear of any gods, speak there against Illuriel, god of King Darniak." This is dramatic speech that is truly exalted and noble. The eloquence which is natural to him when he speaks of imaginative things and which may be his by inheritance has its finest expression in the speeches in his plays.

We are all fictionists nowadays: Lord Dunsany, however, is that rare creature in literature, the fabulist. He does not aim at imposing forms on what we call reality—graceful, impressive or significant forms: he aims at transporting us from this reality altogether. He is like the man who comes to the hunters' lodges and says "You wonder at the moon. I will tell you how the moon was made and why." And having told them about the moon he goes on to tell them about marvellous cities that are beyond the forest and about the jewel that is in the unicorn's horn. If such a one were rebuked for filling the folk with dreams and idle tales, he might (had he the philosophy) make reply: "I have kept alive their spirit of wonder, and wonder in man is holy." Lord Dunsany speaking for himself would say with Blake "Imagination is the man." He would, I think, go on to declare that the one thing worth doing for mankind is to make their imaginations more and more exalted. One can hardly detect a social idea in his work. There is one there, however. It is one of unrelenting hostility to everything that impoverishes man's imagination—to mean cities, to commercial interests, to a culture that arises out of material organization. He dwells forever upon things that arouse the imagination—upon swords and cities, upon temples and palaces, upon slaves in their revolt and kings in their unhappiness. He has the mind of a myth-maker, and he can give ships and cities and whirlpools vast and proper shapes.

It is easy to find his literary origins—they are the Bible, Homer and Herodotus. He made the Bible his book of wonder when he was young, being induced to do this by a censorship his mother had set up—she was adverse, as he tells us, to his reading newspapers and current periodicals. From the Bible he has got his rhythmic, exalted prose. He took from it too the themes that he has so often repeated—fair and unbelieving cities with their prophets and their heathen kings. Homer he loves and often repeats, and the accounts of early civilizations that Herodotus gives delights him. I do not think he reads much modern literature, and I am certain that he reads none of the philosophic, sociological and economic works that fill the bookshops to-day. He would not judge a book by its cover, but he would, I am sure, judge it by its title. I have seen him become enraptured by titles of two books that were being reviewed at the time. One was "The High Deeds of Finn," and the other "The History of the East Roman Empire from the Accession of Irene to the Fall of Basil the Third" (I am not sure I have got the Byzantine sovereigns in right). He has a prodigal imagination. I have watched him sketch a scenario for a play, write a little story, and invent a dozen incidents for tales, in the course of a morning, all the time talking imaginatively. He thinks best, I imagine, in the open air while he is shooting or hunting around his Castle. And he exercises a very gracious hospitality in that twelfth century castle of his in the County Meath, and he would travel a long way a-foot, I know, to find a good talker that he could bring into the circle. It is a long time now since an ancient historian in Ireland wrote into "The Annals of the Four Masters," "There be two great robber barons on the road to Drogheda, Dunsany and Fingall; and if you save yourself from the hands of Fingall, you will assuredly fall into the hands of Dunsany."

PADRAIC COLUM.

NEW YORK, August, 1917.

A DREAMER'S TALES

and

OTHER STORIES

A DREAMER'S TALES

POLTARNEES, BEHOLDER OF OCEAN

TOLDEES, Mondath, Arizim, these are the Inner Lands, the lands whose sentinels upon their borders do not behold the sea. Beyond them to the east there lies a desert, for ever untroubled by man: all yellow it is, and spotted with shadows of stones, and Death is in it, like a leopard lying in the sun. To the south they are bounded by magic, to the west by a mountain, and to the north by the voice and anger of the Polar wind. Like a great wall is the mountain to the west. It comes up out of the distance and goes down into the distance again, and it is named Poltarnees, Beholder of Ocean. To the northward red rocks, smooth and bare of soil, and without any speck of moss or herbage, slope up to the very lips of the Polar wind, and there is nothing else there but the noise of his anger. Very peaceful are the Inner Lands, and very fair are their cities, and there is no war among them, but quiet and ease. And they have no enemy but age, for thirst and fever lie sunning themselves out in the mid-desert, and never prowl into the Inner Lands. And the ghouls and ghosts, whose highway is the night, are kept in the south by the boundary of magic. And very small are all their pleasant cities, and all men are known to one another therein, and bless one another by name as they meet in the streets. And they have a broad, green way in every city that comes in out of some vale or wood or downland, and wanders in and out about the city between the houses and across the streets; and the people walk along it never at all, but every year at her appointed time Spring walks along it from the flowery lands, causing the anemone to bloom on the green way and all the early joys of hidden woods, or deep, secluded vales, or triumphant downlands, whose heads lift up so proudly, far up aloof from cities.

Sometimes waggoners or shepherds walk along this way, they that have come into the city from over cloudy ridges, and the townsmen hinder them not, for there is a tread that troubleth the grass and a tread that troubleth it not, and each man in his own heart knoweth which tread he hath. And in the sunlit spaces of the weald and in the wold's dark places, afar from the music of cities and from the dance of the cities afar, they make there the music of the country places and dance the country dance. Amiable, near and friendly appears to these men the sun, and he is genial to them and tends their younger vines, so they are kind to the little woodland things and any rumour of the fairies or old legend. And when the light of some little distant city makes a slight flush upon the edge of the sky, and the happy golden windows of the homesteads stare gleaming into the dark, then the old and holy figure of Romance, cloaked even to the face, comes down out of hilly woodlands and bids dark shadows to rise and dance, and sends the forest creatures forth to prowl, and lights in a moment in her bower of grass the little glow-worm's lamp, and brings a hush down over the grey lands, and out of it rises faintly on far-off hills the voice of a lute. There are not in the world lands more prosperous and happy than Toldees, Mondath, Arizim.

From these three little kingdoms that are named the Inner Lands the young men stole constantly away. One by one they went, and no one knew why they went save that they had a longing to behold the Sea. Of this longing they spoke little, but a young man would become silent for a few days, and then, one morning very early, he would slip away and slowly climb Poltarnees's difficult slope, and having attained the top pass over and never return. A few stayed behind in the Inner Lands and became old men, but none that had ever climbed Poltarnees from the very earliest times had ever come back again. Many had gone up Poltarnees sworn to return. Once a king sent all his courtiers, one by one, to report the mystery to him, and then went himself; none ever returned.

Now, it was the wont of the folk of the Inner Lands to worship rumours and legends of the Sea, and all that their prophets discovered of the Sea was writ in a sacred book, and with deep devotion on days of festival or mourning read in he temples by the priests. Now, all their temples lay open to the west, resting upon pillars, that the breeze from the Sea might enter them, and they lay open on pillars to the east that the breezes of the Sea might not be hindered but pass onward wherever the Sea list. And this is the legend that they had of the Sea, whom none in the Inner Lands had ever beholden. They say that the Sea is a river heading towards Hercules, and they say that he touches against the edge of the world, and that Poltarnees looks upon him. They say that all the worlds of heaven go bobbing on this river and are swept down with the stream, and that Infinity is thick and furry with forests through which the river in his course sweeps on with all the worlds of heaven. Among the colossal trunks of those dark trees, the smallest fronds of whose branches are many nights, there walk the gods. And whenever its thirst, glowing in space like a great sun, comes upon the beast, the tiger of the gods creeps down to the river to drink. And the tiger of the gods drinks his fill loudly, whelming worlds the while, and the level of the river sinks between its banks ere the beast's thirst is quenched and ceases to glow like a sun. And many worlds thereby are heaped up

dry and stranded, and the gods walk not among them evermore, because they are hard to their feet. These are the
worlds that have no destiny, whose people know no god.
And the river sweeps onwards ever. And the name of the
river is Oriathon, but men call it Ocean. This is the Lower
Faith of the Inner Lands. And there is a Higher Faith which
is not told to all. According to the Higher Faith of the
Inner Lands the river Oriathon sweeps on through the forests of Infinity and all at once falls roaring over an Edge,
whence Time has long ago recalled his hours to fight in his
war with the gods; and falls unlit by the flash of nights and
days, with his flood unmeasured by miles, into the deeps of
nothing.

Now as the centuries went by and the one way by which
a man could climb Poltarnees became worn with feet, more
and more men surmounted it, not to return. And still they
knew not in the Inner Lands upon what mystery Poltarnees
looked. For on a still day and windless, while men walked
happily about their beautiful streets or tended flocks in the
country, suddenly the west wind would bestir himself and
come in from the Sea. And he would come cloaked and
grey and mournful and carry to someone the hungry cry of
the Sea calling out for bones of men. And he that heard
it would move restlessly for some hours, and at last would
rise suddenly, irresistibly up, setting his face to Poltarnees,
and would say, as is the custom of those lands when men
part briefly, "Till a man's heart remembereth," which means
"Farewell for a while;" but those that loved him, seeing his
eyes on Poltarnees, would answer sadly, "Till the gods forget," which means "Farewell."

Now the King of Arizim had a daughter who played with
the wild wood flowers, and with the fountains in her father's
court, and with the little blue heaven-birds that came to her
doorway in the winter to shelter from the snow. And she was
more beautiful than the wild wood flowers, or than all the
fountains in her father's court, or than the blue heaven-birds

in their full winter plumage when they shelter from the snow. The old wise kings of Mondath and of Toldees saw her once as she went lightly down the little paths of her garden, and, turning their gaze into the mists of thought, pondered the destiny of their Inner Lands. And they watched her closely by the stately flowers, and standing alone in the sunlight, and passing and repassing the strutting purple birds that the king's fowlers had brought from Asagéhon. When she was of the age of fifteen years the King of Mondath called a council of kings. And there met with him the kings of Toldees and Arizim. And the King of Mondath in his Council said:

"The call of the unappeased and hungry Sea (and at the word 'Sea' the three kings bowed their heads) lures every year out of our happy kingdoms more and more of our men, and still we know not the mystery of the Sea, and no devised oath has brought one man back. Now thy daughter, Arizim, is lovelier than the sunlight, and lovelier than those stately flowers of thine that stand so tall in her garden, and hath more grace and beauty than those strange birds that the venturous fowlers bring in creaking waggons out of Asagéhon, whose feathers are alternate purple and white. Now, he that shall love thy daughter, Hilnaric, whoever he shall be, is the man to climb Poltarnees and return, as none hath ever before, and tell us upon what Poltarnees looks; for it may be that thy daughter is more beautiful than the Sea."

Then from his Seat of Council arose the King of Arizim. He said: "I fear that thou hast spoken blasphemy against the Sea, and I have a dread that ill will come of it. Indeed I had not thought she was so fair. It is such a short while ago that she was quite a small child with her hair still unkempt and not yet attired in the manner of princesses, and she would go up into the wild woods unattended and come back with her robes unseemly and all torn, and would not take reproof with humble spirit, but made grimaces even in my marble court all set about with fountains."

Then said the King of Toldees:

"Let us watch more closely and let us see the Princess Hilnaric in the season of the orchard-bloom when the great birds go by that know the Sea, to rest in our inland places; and if she be more beautiful than the sunrise over our folded kingdoms when all the orchards bloom, it may be that she is more beautiful than the Sea."

And the King of Arizim said:

"I fear this is terrible blasphemy, yet will I do as you have decided in council."

And the season of the orchard-bloom appeared. One night the King of Arizim called his daughter forth on to his outer balcony of marble. And the moon was rising huge and round and holy over dark woods, and all the fountains were singing to the night. And the moon touched the marble palace gables, and they glowed in the land. And the moon touched the heads of all the fountains, and the grey columns broke into fairy lights. And the moon left the dark ways of the forest and lit the whole white palace and its fountains and shone on the forehead of the Princess, and the palace of Arizim glowed afar, and the fountains became columns of gleaming jewels and song. And the moon made a music at his rising, but it fell a little short of mortal ears. And Hilnaric stood there wondering, clad in white, with the moonlight shining on her forehead; and watching her from the shadows on the terrace stood the kings of Mondath and Toldees. They said:

"She is more beautiful than the moon-rise."

And on another day the King of Arizim bade his daughter forth at dawn, and they stood again upon the balcony. And the sun came up over a world of orchards, and the sea-mists went back over Poltarnees to the Sea; little wild voices arose in all the thickets, the voices of the fountains began to die, and the song arose, in all the marble temples, of the birds that are sacred to the Sea. And Hilnaric stood there, still glowing with dreams of heaven.

"She is more beautiful," said the kings, "than morning."

Yet one more trial they made of Hilnaric's beauty, for they watched her on the terraces at sunset ere yet the petals of the orchards had fallen, and all along the edge of neighbouring woods the rhododendron was blooming with the azalea. And the sun went down under craggy Poltarnees, and the sea-mist poured over his summit inland. And the marble temples stood up clear in the evening, but films of twilight were drawn between the mountain and the city. Then from the Temple ledges and eaves of palaces the bats fell headlong downwards, then spread their wings and floated up and down through darkening ways; lights came blinking out in golden windows, men cloaked themselves against the grey sea-mist, the sound of small songs arose, and the face of Hilnaric became a resting-place for mysteries and dreams.

"Than all these things," said the kings, "she is more lovely: but who can say whether she is lovelier than the Sea?"

Prone in a rhododendron thicket at the edge of the palace lawns a hunter had waited since the sun went down. Near to him was a deep pool where the hyacinths grew and strange flowers floated upon it with broad leaves, and there the great bull gariachs came down to drink by starlight, and, waiting there for the gariachs to come, he saw the white form of the Princess leaning on her balcony. Before the stars shone out or the bulls came down to drink he left his lurking-place and moved closer to the palace to see more nearly the Princess. The palace lawns were full of untrodden dew, and everything was still when he came across them, holding his great spear. In the farthest corner of the terraces the three old kings were discussing the beauty of Hilnaric and the destiny of the Inner Lands. Moving lightly, with a hunter's tread, the watcher by the pool came very near, even in the still evening, before the Princess saw him. When he saw her closely he exclaimed suddenly:

"She must be more beautiful than the Sea."

When the Princess turned and saw his garb and his great spear she knew that he was a hunter of gariachs.

When the three kings heard the young man exclaim they said softly to one another:

"This must be the man."

Then they revealed themselves to him, and spoke to him to try him. They said:

"Sir, you have spoken blasphemy against the Sea."

And the young man muttered:

"She is more beautiful than the Sea."

And the kings said:

"We are older than you and wiser, and know that nothing is more beautiful than the Sea."

And the young man took off the gear of his head, and became downcast, and knew that he spake with kings, yet he answered:

"By this spear, she is more beautiful than the Sea."

And all the while the Princess stared at him, knowing him to be a hunter of gariachs.

Then the King of Arizim said to the watcher by the pool:

"If thou wilt go up Poltarnees and come back, as none have come, and report to us what lure or magic is in the Sea, we will pardon thy blasphemy, and thou shalt have the Princess to wife and sit among the Council of the Kings."

And gladly thereunto the young man consented. And the Princess spoke to him, and asked him his name. And he told her that his name was Athelvok, and great joy arose in him at the sound of her voice. And to the three kings he promised to set out on the third day to scale the slope of Poltarnees and to return again, and this was the oath by which they bound him to return:

"I swear by the Sea that bears the worlds away, by the river of Oriathon, which men call Ocean, and by the gods and their tiger, and by the doom of the worlds, that I will return again to the Inner Lands, having beheld the Sea."

And that oath he swore with solemnity that very night in

one of the temples of the Sea, but the three kings trusted
more to the beauty of Hilnaric even than to the power of
the oath.

The next day Athelvok came to the palace of Arizim with
the morning, over the fields to the East and out of the country of Toldees, and Hilnaric came out along her balcony and
met him on the terraces. And she asked him if he had ever
slain a gariach, and he said that he had slain three, and then
he told her how he had killed his first down by the pool in
the wood. For he had taken his father's spear and gone
down to the edge of the pool, and had lain under the azaleas
there waiting for the stars to shine, by whose first light the
gariachs go to the pools to drink; and he had gone too early
and had had long to wait, and the passing hours seemed
longer than they were. And all the birds came in that home
at night, and the bat was abroad, and the hour of the duck
went by, and still no gariach came down to the pool; and
Athelvok felt sure that none would come. And just as this
grew to a certainty in his mind the thicket parted noiselessly
and a huge bull gariach stood facing him on the edge of the
water, and his great horns swept out sideways from his head,
and at the ends curved upwards, and were four strides in
width from tip to tip. And he had not seen Athelvok, for the
great bull was on the far side of the little pool, and Athelvok
could not creep round to him for fear of meeting the wind
(for the gariachs, who can see little in the dark forests, rely
on hearing and smell). But he devised swiftly in his mind
while the bull stood there with head erect just twenty strides
from him across the water. And the bull sniffed the wind
cautiously and listened, then lowered its great head down to
the pool and drank. At that instant Athelvok leapt into the
water and shot forward through its weedy depths among
the stems of the strange flowers that floated upon broad
leaves on the surface. And Athelvok kept his spear out
straight before him, and the fingers of his left hand he held
rigid and straight, not pointing upwards, and so did not come

to the surface, but was carried onward by the strength of his spring and passed unentangled through the stems of the flowers. When Athelvok jumped into the water the bull must have thrown his head up, startled at the splash, then he would have listened and have sniffed the air, and neither hearing nor scenting any danger he must have remained rigid for some moments, for it was in that attitude that Athelvok found him as he emerged breathless at his feet. And, striking at once, Athelvok drove the spear into his throat before the head and the terrible horns came down. But Athelvok had clung to one of the great horns, and had been carried at terrible speed through the rhodendron bushes until the gariach fell, but rose at once again, and died standing up, still struggling, drowned in its own blood.

But to Hilnaric listening it was as though one of the heroes of old time had come back again in the full glory of his legendary youth.

And long time they went up and down the terraces, saying those things which were said before and since, and which lips shall yet be made to say again. And above them stood Poltarnees beholding the Sea.

And the day came when Athelvok should go. And Hilnaric said to him:

"Will you not indeed most surely come back again, having just looked over the summit of Poltarnees?"

Athelvok answered: "I will indeed come back, for thy voice is more beautiful than the hymn of the priests when they chant and praise the Sea, and though many tributary seas ran down into Oriathon and he and all the others poured their beauty into one pool below me, yet would I return swearing that thou wert fairer than they."

And Hilnaric answered:

"The wisdom of my heart tells me, or old knowledge or prophecy, or strange lore, that I shall never hear thy voice again. And for this I give thee my forgiveness."

But he, repeating the oath that he had sworn, set out,

looking often backwards until the slope became too steep
and his face was set to the rock. It was in the morning that
he started, and he climbed all the day with little rest, where
every foot-hole was smooth with many feet. Before he
reached the top the sun disappeared from him, and darker
and darker grew the Inner Lands. Then he pushed on so
as to see before dark whatever thing Poltarnees had to show.
The dusk was deep over the Inner Lands, and the lights of
cities twinkled through the sea-mist when he came to Poltarnees' summit, and the sun before him was not yet gone from
the sky.

And there below him was the old wrinkled Sea, smiling
and murmuring song. And he nursed little ships with gleaming sails, and in his hands were old regretted wrecks, and
masts all studded over with golden nails that he had rent
in anger out of beautiful galleons. And the glory of the sun
was among the surges as they brought driftwood out of isles
of spice, tossing their golden heads. And the grey currents
crept away to the south like companionless serpents that love
something afar with a restless, deadly love. And the whole
plain of water glittering with late sunlight, and the surges
and the currents and the white sails of ships were all together
like the face of a strange new god that has looked a man for
the first time in the eyes at the moment of his death; and
Athelvok, looking on the wonderful Sea, knew why it was
that the dead never return, for there is something that the
dead feel and know, and the living would never understand
even though the dead should come and speak to them about
it. And there was the Sea smiling at him, glad with the glory
of the sun. And there was a haven there for homing ships,
and a sunlit city stood upon its marge, and people walked
about the streets of it clad in the unimagined merchandise of
far sea-bordering lands.

An easy slope of loose crumbled rock went from the top
of Poltarnees to the shore of the Sea.

For a long while Athelvok stood there regretfully, knowing

that there had come something into his soul that no one in
the Inner Lands could understand, where the thoughts of
their minds had gone no farther than the three little kingdoms. Then, looking long upon the wandering ships, and the
marvellous merchandise from alien lands, and the unknown
colour that wreathed the brows of the Sea, he turned his face
to the darkness and the Inner Lands.

At that moment the Sea sang a dirge at sunset for all the
harm that he had done in anger and all the ruin wrought on
adventurous ships; and there were tears in the voice of the
tyrannous Sea, for he had loved the galleons that he had
overwhelmed, and he called all men to him and all living
things that he might make amends, because he had loved the
bones that he had strewn afar. And Athelvok turned and
set one foot upon the crumbled slope, and then another, and
walked a little way to be nearer to the Sea, and then a dream
came upon him and he felt that men had wronged the lovely
Sea because he had been angry a little, because he had been
sometimes cruel; he felt that there was trouble among the
tides of the Sea because he had loved the galleons who were
dead. Still he walked on and the crumbled stones rolled
with him, and just as the twilight faded and a star appeared
he came to the golden shore, and walked on till the surges
were about his knees, and he heard the prayer-like blessings
of the Sea. Long he stood thus, while the stars came out
above him and shone again in the surges; more stars came
wheeling in their courses up from the Sea, lights twinkled
out through all the haven city, lanterns were slung from the
ships, the purple night burned on; and Earth, to the eyes
of the gods as they sat afar, glowed as with one flame. Then
Athelvok went into the haven city; there he met many who
had left the Inner Lands before him; none of them wished
to return to the people who had not seen the Sea; many of
them had forgotten the three little kingdoms, and it was
rumoured that one man, who had once tried to return, had
found the shifting, crumbling slope impossible to climb.

Hilnaric never married. But her dowry was set aside to build a temple wherein men curse the ocean.

Once every year, with solemn rite and ceremony, they curse the tides of the Sea; and the moon looks in and hates them.

BLAGDAROSS

O N a waste place strewn with bricks in the outskirts of a town twilight was falling. A star or two appeared over the smoke, and distant windows lit mysterious lights. The stillness deepened and the loneliness. Then all the outcast things that are silent by day found voices.

An old cork spoke first. He said: "I grew in Andalusian woods, but never listened to the idle songs of Spain. I only grew strong in the sunlight waiting for my destiny. One day the merchants came and took us away and carried us all along the shore of the sea, piled high on the backs of donkeys, and in a town by the sea they made me into the shape that I am now. One day they sent me northward to Provence, and there I fulfilled my destiny. For they set me as a guard over the bubbling wine, and I faithfully stood sentinel for twenty years. For the first few years in the bottle that I guarded the wine slept, dreaming of Provence; but as the years went on he grew stronger and stronger, until at last whenever a man went by the wine would put out all his might against me, saying: 'Let me go free; let me go free!' And every year his strength increased, and he grew more clamorous when men went by, but never availed to hurl me from my post. But when I had powerfully held him for twenty years they brought him to the banquet and took me from my post, and the wine arose rejoicing and leapt through the veins of men and exalted their souls within them till they stood up in their places and sang Provençal songs. But me they cast away—me that had been sentinel for twenty years,

14

and was still as strong and staunch as when first I went on guard. Now I am an outcast in a cold northern city, who once have known the Andalusian skies and guarded long ago Provençal suns that swam in the heart of the rejoicing wine."

An unstruck match that somebody had dropped spoke next. "I am a child of the sun," he said, "and an enemy of cities; there is more in my heart than you know of. I am a brother of Etna and Stromboli; I have fires lurking in me that will one day rise up beautiful and strong. We will not go into servitude on any hearth nor work machines for our food, but we will take our own food where we find it on that day when we are strong. There are wonderful children in my heart whose faces shall be more lively than the rainbow; they shall make a compact with the North wind, and he shall lead them forth; all shall be black behind them and black above them, and there shall be nothing beautiful in the world but them; they shall seize upon the earth and it shall be theirs, and nothing shall stop them but our old enemy the sea."

Then an old broken kettle spoke, and said: "I am the friend of cities. I sit among the slaves upon the hearth, the little flames that have been fed with coal. When the slaves dance behind the iron bars I sit in the middle of the dance and sing and make our masters glad. And I make songs about the comfort of the cat, and about the malice that is towards her in the heart of the dog, and about the crawling of the baby, and about the ease that is in the lord of the house when we brew the good brown tea; and sometimes when the house is very warm and slaves and masters are glad, I rebuke the hostile winds that prowl about the world."

And then there spoke the piece of an old cord. "I was made in a place of doom, and doomed men made my fibres, working without hope. Therefore there came a grimness into my heart, so that I never let anything go free when once I was set to bind it. Many a thing have I bound relentlessly for months and for years; for I used to come coiling into warehouses where the great boxes lay all open to the air, and one of them would be suddenly closed up, and my fearful strength would be set on him like a curse, and if his timbers groaned when first I seized them, or if they creaked aloud in the lonely night, thinking of woodlands out of which they came, then I only gripped them tighter still, for the poor useless hate is in my soul of those that made me in the place of doom. Yet, for all the things that my prison-clutch has held, the last work that I did was to set something free. I lay idle one night in the gloom on the warehouse floor. Nothing stirred there, and even the spider slept. Towards midnight a great flock of echoes suddenly leapt up from the wooden planks and circled round the roof. A man was coming towards me all alone. And as he came his soul was reproaching him, and I saw that there was a great trouble between the man and his soul, for his soul would not let him be, but went on reproaching him.

"Then the man saw me and said, 'This at least will not fail me.' When I heard him say this about me, I determined that whatever he might require of me it should be done to the uttermost. And as I made this determination in my un-altering heart, he picked me up and stood on an empty box that I should have bound on the morrow, and tied one end of me to a dark rafter; and the knot was carelessly tied, because his soul was reproaching him all the while continually and giving him no ease. Then he made the other end of me into a noose, but when the man's soul saw this it stopped reproaching the man, and cried out to him hurriedly, and besought him to be at peace with it and to do nothing sudden; but the man went on with his work, and put the noose down over his face and underneath his chin, and the soul screamed horribly.

"Then the man kicked the box away with his foot, and the moment he did this I knew that my strength was not great enough to hold him; but I remembered that he had said I would not fail him, and I put all my grim vigour into my fibres and held him by sheer will. Then the soul shouted to me to give way, but I said:

" 'No; you vexed the man.'

"Then it screamed to me to leave go of the rafter, and already I was slipping, for I only held on to it by a careless knot, but I gripped with my prison grip and said:

" 'You vexed the man.'

"And very swiftly it said other things to me, but I answered not; and at last the soul that vexed the man that had trusted me flew away and left him at peace. I was never able to bind things any more, for every one of my fibres was worn and wrenched, and even my relentless heart was weakened by the struggle. Very soon afterwards I was thrown out here. I have done my work."

So they spoke among themselves, but all the while there loomed above them the form of an old rocking-horse complaining bitterly. He said: "I am Blagdaross. Woe is me that I should lie now an outcast among these worthy but little people. Alas! for the days that are gathered, and alas for the Great One that was a master and a soul to me, whose spirit is now shrunken and can never know me again, and no more ride abroad on knightly quests. I was Bucephalus when he was Alexander, and carried him victorious as far as Ind. I encountered dragons with him when he was St. George, I was the horse of Roland fighting for Christendom, and was often Rosinante. I fought in tournays and went errant upon quests, and met Ulysses and the heroes and the fairies. Or late in the evening, just before the lamps in the nursery were put out, he would suddenly mount me, and we would gallop through Africa. There we would pass by night through tropic forests, and come upon dark rivers sweeping by, all gleaming with the eyes of crocodiles, where the hippopotamus floated down the stream, and mysterious craft loomed suddenly out of the dark and furtively passed away. And when we had passed through the forest lit by the fireflies we would come to the open plains, and gallop onwards wit'

scarlet flamingoes flying along beside us through the lands
of dusky kings, with golden crowns upon their heads and
sceptres in their hands, who came running out of their palaces to see us pass. Then I would wheel suddenly, and the
dust flew up from my four hoofs as I turned and we gal-
loped home again, and my master was put to bed. And
again he would ride abroad on another day till we came to
magical fortresses guarded by wizardry and overthrew the
dragons at the gate, and ever came back with a princess
fairer than the sea.

"But my master began to grow larger in his body and
smaller in his soul, and then he rode more seldom upon
quests. At last he saw gold and never came again, and I
was cast out here among these little people."

But while the rocking-horse was speaking two boys stole
away, unnoticed by their parents, from a house on the edge
of the waste place, and were coming across it looking for
adventures. One of them carried a broom, and when he saw
the rocking-horse he said nothing, but broke off the handle
from the broom and thrust it between his braces and his
shirt on the left side. Then he mounted the rocking-horse,
and drawing forth the broomstick, which was sharp and
spiky at the end, said, "Saladin is in this desert with all
his paynims, and I am Cœur de Lion." After a while the
other boy said: "Now let me kill Saladin too." But Blagdaross in his wooden heart, that exulted with thoughts of battle, said: "I am Blagdaross yet!"

THE MADNESS OF ANDELSPRUTZ

I FIRST saw the city of Andelsprutz on an afternoon in spring. The day was full of sunshine as I came by the way of the fields, and all that morning I had said, "There will be sunlight on it when I see for the first time the beautiful conquered city whose fame has so often made for me lovely dreams." Suddenly I saw its fortifications lifting out of the fields, and behind them stood its belfries. I went in by a gate and saw its houses and streets, and a great disappointment came upon me. For there is an air about a city, and it has a way with it, whereby a man may recognize one from another at once. There are cities full of happiness and cities full of pleasure, and cities full of gloom. There are cities with their faces to heaven, and some with their faces to earth; some have a way of looking at the past and others look at the future; some notice you if you come among them, others glance at you, others let you go by. Some love the cities that are their neighbours, others are dear to the plains and to the heath; some cities are bare to the wind, others have purple cloaks and others brown cloaks, and some are clad in white. Some tell the old tale of their infancy, with others it is secret; some cities sing and some mutter, some are angry, and some have broken hearts, and each city has her way of greeting Time.

I had said: "I will see Andelsprutz arrogant with her beauty," and I had said: "I will see her weeping over her conquest."

I had said: "She will sing songs to me," and "she will be reticent," "she will be all robed," and "she will be bare but splendid."

But the windows of Andelsprutz in her houses looked vacantly over the plains like the eyes of a dead madman. At the hour her chimes sounded unlovely and discordant, some of them were out of tune, and the bells of some were cracked, her roofs were bald and without moss. At evening no pleasant rumour arose in her streets. When the lamps were lit in the houses no mystical flood of light stole out into the dusk, you merely saw that there were lighted lamps; Andelsprutz had no way with her and no air about her. When the night fell and the blinds were all drawn down, then I perceived what I had not thought in the daylight. I knew then that Andelsprutz was dead.

I saw a fair-haired man who drank beer in a café, and I said to him:

"Why is the city of Andelsprutz quite dead, and her soul gone hence?"

He answered: "Cities do not have souls and there is never any life in bricks."

And I said to him: "Sir, you have spoken truly."

And I asked the same question of another man, and he gave me the same answer, and I thanked him for his courtesy. And I saw a man of a more slender build, who had black hair, and channels in his cheeks for tears to run in, and I said to him:

"Why is Andelsprutz quite dead, and when did her soul go hence?"

And he answered: "Andelsprutz hoped too much. For thirty years would she stretch out her arms toward the land of Akla every night, to Mother Akla from whom she had been stolen. Every night she would be hoping and sighing, and stretching out her arms to Mother Akla. At midnight, once a year, on the anniversary of the terrible day, Akla would send spies to lay a wreath against the walls of Andelsprutz. She could do no more. And on this night, once in every year, I used to weep, for weeping was the mood of the city that nursed me. Every night while other cities slept did Andelsprutz sit brooding here and hoping, till thirty wreaths lay mouldering by her walls, and still the armies of Akla could not come.

"But after she had hoped so long, and on the night that faithful spies had brought the thirtieth wreath, Andelsprutz went suddenly mad. All the bells clanged hideously in the belfries, horses bolted in the streets, the dogs all howled, the stolid conquerors awoke and turned in their beds and slept again; and I saw the grey shadowy form of Andelsprutz rise up, decking her hair with the phantasms of cathedrals, and stride away from her city. And the great shadowy form that was the soul of Andelsprutz went away muttering to the mountains, and there I followed her—for had she not been my nurse? Yes, I went away alone into the mountains, and for three days, wrapped in a cloak, I slept in their misty solitudes. I had no food to eat, and to drink I had only the water of the mountain streams. By day no living thing was near to me, and I heard nothing but the noise of the wind, and the mountain streams roaring. But for three nights I heard all round me on the mountain the sounds of a great city: I saw the lights of tall cathedral windows flash momently on the peaks, and at times the glimmering lantern of some fortress patrol. And I saw the huge misty outline of the soul of Andelsprutz sitting decked with her ghostly cathedrals, speaking to herself, with her eyes fixed before her in a mad stare, telling of ancient wars. And her confused speech for all those nights upon the mountain was sometimes the voice of traffic, and then of church bells, and then of the bugles, but oftenest it was the voice of red war; and it was all incoherent, and she was quite mad.

"The third night it rained heavily all night long, but I stayed up there to watch the soul of my native city. And she still sat staring straight before her, raving; but her voice was gentler now, there were more chimes in it, and occasional song. Midnight passed, and the rain still swept down on me, and still the solitudes of the mountain were full of the mutterings of the poor mad city. And the hours after midnight came, the cold hours wherein sick men die.

"Suddenly I was aware of great shapes moving in the rain, and heard the sound of voices that were not of my city nor yet of any that I ever knew. And presently I discerned, though faintly, the souls of a great concourse of cities, all bending over Andelsprutz and comforting her, and the ravines of the mountains roared that night with the voices of cities that had lain still for centuries. For there came the soul of Camelot that had so long ago forsaken Usk; and there was Ilion, all girt with towers, still cursing the sweet face of ruinous Helen; I saw there Babylon and Persepolis, and the bearded face of bull-like Ninevah, and Athens mourning her immortal gods.

"All these souls of cities that were dead spoke that night on the mountain to my city and soothed her, until at last she muttered of war no longer, and her eyes stared wildly no more, but she hid her face in her hands and for some while wept softly. At last she arose, and, walking slowly and with bended head, and leaning upon Ilion and Carthage, went mournfully eastwards; and the dust of her highways swirled behind her as she went, a ghostly dust that never turned to mud in all that drenching rain. And so the souls of the cities led her away, and gradually they disappeared from the mountain, and the ancient voices died away in the distance.

"Never since then have I seen my city alive; but once I met with a traveller who said that somewhere in the midst of a great desert are gathered together the souls of all dead cities. He said that he was lost once in a place where there was no water, and he heard their voices speaking all the night."

But I said: "I was once without water in a desert and heard a city speaking to me, but knew not whether it really spoke or not, for on that day I heard so many terrible things, and only some of them were true."

And the man with the black hair said: "I believe it to be true, though whither she went I know not. I only know that a shepherd found me in the morning faint with hunger and cold, and carried me down here; and when I came to Andelsprutz it was, as you have perceived it, dead."

WHERE THE TIDES EBB AND FLOW

I DREAMT that I had done a horrible thing, so that burial was to be denied me either in soil or sea, neither could there be any hell for me.

I waited for some hours, knowing this. Then my friends came for me, and slew me secretly and with ancient rite, and lit great tapers, and carried me away.

It was all in London that the thing was done, and they went furtively at dead of night along grey streets and among mean houses until they came to the river. And the river and the tide of the sea were grappling with one another between the mud-banks, and both of them were black and full of lights. A sudden wonder came into the eyes of each, as my friends came near to them with their glaring tapers. All these things I saw as they carried me, dead and stiffening, for my soul was still among my bones, because there was no hell for it, because Christian burial was denied me.

They took me down a stairway that was green with slimy things, and so came slowly to the terrible mud. There, in the territory of forsaken things, they dug a shallow grave. When they had finished they laid me in the grave, and suddenly they cast their tapers to the river. And when the water had quenched the flaring lights the tapers looked pale and small as they bobbed upon the tide, and at once the glamour of the calamity was gone, and I noticed then the approach of the huge dawn; and my friends cast their cloaks over their faces, and the solemn procession was turned into many fugitives that furtively stole away.

Then the mud came back wearily and covered all but my face. There I lay alone with quite forgotten things, with drifting things that the tides will take no farther, with useless things and lost things, and with the horrible unnatural bricks that are neither stone nor soil. I was rid of feeling, because I had been killed, but perception and thought were in my unhappy soul. The dawn widened, and I saw the desolate houses that crowded the marge of the river, and their dead windows peered into my dead eyes, windows with bales behind them instead of human souls. I grew so weary looking at these forlorn things that I wanted to cry out, but could not, because I was dead. Then I knew, as I had never known before, that for all the years that herd of desolate houses had wanted to cry out too, but, being dead, were dumb. And I knew then that it had yet been well with the forgotten drifting things if they had wept, but they were eyeless and without life. And I, too, tried to weep, but there were no tears in my dead eyes. And I knew then that the river might have cared for us, might have caressed us, might have sung to us, but he swept broadly onwards, thinking of nothing but the princely ships.

At last the tide did what the river would not, and came and covered me over, and my soul had rest in the green water, and rejoiced and believed that it had the Burial of the Sea. But with the ebb the water fell again, and left me alone again with the callous mud among the forgotten things that drift no more, and with the sight of all those desolate houses, and with the knowledge among all of us that each was dead.

In the mournful wall behind me, hung with green weeds, forsaken of the sea, dark tunnels appeared, and secret narrow passages that were clamped and barred. From these at last the stealthy rats came down to nibble me away, and my soul rejoiced thereat and believed that he would be free perforce from the accursed bones to which burial was refused. Very soon the rats ran away a little space and whispered among themselves. They never came any more. When I found that I was accursed even among the rats I tried to weep again.

Then the tide came swinging back and covered the dreadful mud, and hid the desolate houses, and soothed the forgotten things, and my soul had ease for a while in the sepulture of the sea. And then the tide forsook me again.

To and fro it came about me for many years. Then the County Council found me, and gave me decent burial. It was the first grave that I had ever slept in. That very night my friends came for me. They dug me up and put me back again in the shallow hole in the mud.

Again and again through the years my bones found burial, but always behind the funeral lurked one of those terrible men who, as soon as night fell, came and dug them up and carried them back again to the hole in the mud.

And then one day the last of those men died who once had done to me this terrible thing. I heard his soul go over the river at sunset.

And again I hoped.

A few weeks afterwards I was found once more, and once more taken out of that restless place and given deep burial in sacred ground, where my soul hoped that it should rest.

Almost at once men came with cloaks and tapers to give me back to the mud, for the thing had become a tradition and a rite. And all the forsaken things mocked me in their dumb hearts when they saw me carried back, for they were jealous of me because I had left the mud. It must be remembered that I could not weep.

And the years went by seawards where the black barges go, and the great derelict centuries became lost at sea, and still I lay there without any cause to hope, and daring not to hope without a cause, because of the terrible envy and the anger of the things that could drift no more.

Once a great storm rode up, even as far as London, out of the sea from the South; and he came curving into the river with the fierce East wind. And he was mightier than the dreary tides, and went with great leaps over the listless mud. And all the sad forgotten things rejoiced, and mingled with things that were haughtier than they, and rode once more amongst the lordly shipping that was driven up and down. And out of their hideous home he took my bones, never again, I hoped, to be vexed with the ebb and flow. And with the fall of the tide he went riding down the river and turned to the southwards, and so went to his home. And my bones he scattered among many isles and along the shores of happy alien mainlands. And for a moment, while they were far asunder, my soul was almost free.

Then there arose, at the will of the moon, the assiduous flow of the tide, and it undid at once the work of the ebb, and gathered my bones from the marge of sunny isles, and gleaned them all along the mainland's shores, and went rocking northwards till it came to the mouth of the Thames, and there turned westwards its relentless face, and so went up the river and came to the hole in the mud, and into it dropped my bones; and partly the mud covered them and partly it left them white, for the mud cares not for its forsaken things.

Then the ebb came, and I saw the dead eyes of the houses and the jealousy of the other forgotten things that the storm had not carried thence.

And some more centuries passed over the ebb and flow and over the loneliness of things forgotten. And I lay there all the while in the careless grip of the mud, never wholly covered, yet never able to go free, and I longed for the great caress of the warm Earth or the comfortable lap of the Sea.

Sometimes men found my bones and buried them, but the tradition never died, and my friends' successors always brought them back. At last the barges went no more, and there were fewer lights; shaped timbers no longer floated down the fair-way. and there came instead old wind-uprooted trees in all their natural simplicity.

At last I was aware that somewhere near me a blade of

grass was moving, and the moss began to appear all over the dead houses. One day some thistledown went drifting over the river.

For some years I watched these signs attentively, until I became certain that London was passing away. Then I hoped once more, and all along both banks of the river there was anger among the lost things that anything should dare to hope upon the forsaken mud. Gradually the horrible houses crumbled, until the poor dead things that never had had life got decent burial among the weeds and moss. At last the may appeared and the convolvulus. Finally, the wild rose stood up over mounds that had been wharves and warehouses. Then I knew that the cause of Nature had triumphed, and London had passed away.

The last man in London came to the wall by the river, in an ancient cloak that was one of those that once my friends had worn, and peered over the edge to see that I still was there. Then he went, and I never saw men again: they had passed away with London.

A few days after the last man had gone the birds came into London, all the birds that sing. When they first saw me they all looked sideways at me, then they went away a little and spoke among themselves.

"He only sinned against Man," they said; "it is not our quarrel."

"Let us be kind to him," they said.

Then they hopped nearer me and began to sing. It was the time of the rising of the dawn, and from both banks of the river, and from the sky, and from the thickets that were once the streets, hundreds of birds were singing. As the light increased the birds sang more and more; they grew thicker and thicker in the air above my head, till there were thousands of them singing there, and then millions, and at last I could see nothing but a host of flickering wings with the sunlight on them, and little gaps of sky. Then when there was nothing to be heard in London but the myriad

notes of that exultant song, my soul rose up from the bones
in the hole in the mud and began to climb up the song
heavenwards.   And it seemed that a laneway opened amongst
the wings of the birds, and it went up and up, and one of the
smaller gates of Paradise stood ajar at the end of it.   And
then I knew by a sign that the mud should receive me no
more, for suddenly I found that I could weep.

At this moment I opened my eyes in bed in a house in
London, and outside some sparrows were twittering in a tree
in the light of the radiant morning; and there were tears still
wet upon my face, for one's restraint is feeble while one
sleeps.   But I arose and opened the window wide, and,
stretching my hands out over the little garden, I blessed the
birds whose song had woken me up from the troubled and
terrible centuries of my dream.

BETHMOORA

THERE is a faint freshness in the London night as though
some strayed reveller of a breeze had left his comrades
in the Kentish uplands and had entered the town by stealth.
The pavements are a little damp and shiny. Upon one's
ears that at this late hour have become very acute there
hits the tap of a remote football. Louder and louder grow
the taps, filling the whole night. And a black cloaked figure
passes by, and goes tapping into the dark. One who has
danced goes homewards. Somewhere a ball has closed its
doors and ended. Its yellow lights are out, its musicians are
silent, its dancers have all gone into the night air, and Time
has said of it, "Let it be past and over, and among the things
that I have put away."

Shadows begin to detach themselves from their great
gathering places. No less silently than those shadows that
are thin and dead, move homewards the stealthy cats. Thus
have we even in London our faint forebodings of the dawn's
approach, which the birds and the beasts and the stars are
crying aloud to the untrammelled fields.

At what moment I know not I perceive that the night itself
is irrecoverably overthrown. It is suddenly revealed to me
by the weary pallor of the street lamps that the streets are
silent and nocturnal still, not because there is any strength
in night, but because men have not yet arisen from sleep to
defy him. So have I seen dejected and untidy guards still

bearing antique muskets in palatial gateways, although the realms of the monarch that they guard have shrunk to a single province which no enemy yet has troubled to overrun.

And it is now manifest from the aspect of the street lamps, those abashed dependants of night, that already English mountain peaks have seen the dawn, that the cliffs of Dover are standing white to the morning, that the sea-mist has lifted and is pouring inland.

And now men with a hose have come and are sluicing out the streets.

Behold now night is dead.

What memories, what fancies throng one's mind! A night but just now gathered out of London by the hostile hand of Time. A million common artificial things all cloaked for a while in mystery, like beggars robed in purple, and seated on dread thrones. Four million people asleep, dreaming perhaps. What worlds have they gone into? Whom have they met? But my thoughts are far off with Bethmoora in her loneliness, whose gates swing to and fro. To and fro they swing, and creak and creak in the wind, but no one hears them. They are of green copper, very lovely, but no one sees them now. The desert wind pours sand into their hinges, no watchman comes to ease them. No guard goes round Bethmoora's battlements, no enemy assails them. There are no lights in her houses, no footfall in her streets; she stands there dead and lonely beyond the Hills of Hap, and I would see Bethmoora once again, but dare not.

It is many a year, as they tell me, since Bethmoora became desolate.

Her desolation is spoken of in taverns where sailors meet, and certain travellers have told me of it.

I had hoped to see Bethmoora once again. It is many a year ago, they say, when the vintage was last gathered in from the vineyards that I knew, where it is all desert now. It was a radiant day, and the people of the city were dancing by the vineyards, while here and there one played upon the kalipac. The purple flowering shrubs were all in bloom, and the snow shone upon the Hills of Hap.

Outside the copper gates they crushed the grapes in vats to make the syrabub. It had been a goodly vintage.

In little gardens at the desert's edge men beat the tambang and the tittibuk, and blew melodiously the zootibar.

All there was mirth and song and dance, because the vintage had been gathered in, and there would be ample syrabub for the winter months, and much left over to exchange for turquoises and emeralds with the merchants who come down from Oxuhahn. Thus they rejoiced all day over their vintage on the narrow strip of cultivated ground that lay between Bethmoora and the desert which meets the sky to the South. And when the heat of the day began to abate, and the sun drew near to the snows on the Hills of Hap, the note of the zootibar still rose clear from the gardens, and the brilliant dresses of the dancers still wound among the flowers. All that day three men on mules had been noticed crossing the face of the Hills of Hap. Backwards and forwards they moved as the track wound lower and lower, three little specks of black against the snow. They were seen first in the very early morning up near the shoulder of Peol Jagganoth, and seemed to be coming out of Utnar Véhi. All day they came. And in the evening, just before lights come out and colours change, they appeared before Bethmoora's copper gates. They carried staves, such as messengers bear in those lands, and seemed sombrely clad when the dancers all came round them with their green and lilac dresses. Those Europeans who were present and heard the message given were ignorant of the language, and only caught the name of Utnar Véhi. But it was brief, and passed rapidly from mouth to mouth, and almost at once the people burnt their vineyards and began to flee away from Bethmoora, going for the most part northwards, though some went to the East. They ran down out of their fair white houses, and streamed through the copper gate; the throbbing of the tambang and the tittibuk suddenly ceased with the note of the zootibar, and the clinking kalipac stopped a moment after. The three strange travellers went back the way they came the instant their message was given. It was the hour when a light would have appeared in some high tower, and window after window would have poured into the dusk its lion-frightening light, and the copper gates would have been fastened up. But no lights came out in windows there that night and have not ever since, and those copper gates were left wide and have never shut, and the sound arose of the red fire crackling in the vineyards, and the pattering of feet fleeing softly. There were no cries, no other sounds at all, only the rapid and determined flight. They fled as swiftly and quietly as a herd of wild cattle flee when they suddenly see a man. It was as though something had befallen which had been feared for generations, which could only be escaped by instant flight, which left no time for indecision.

Then fear took the Europeans also, and they too fled. And what the message was I have never heard.

Many believe that it was a message from Thuba Mleen, the mysterious emperor of those lands, who is never seen by man, advising that Bethmoora should be left desolate. Others say that the message was one of warning from the gods, whether from friendly gods or from adverse ones they know not.

And others hold that the Plague was ravaging a line of cities over in Utnar Véhi, following the South-west wind which for many weeks had been blowing across them towards Bethmoora.

Some say that the terrible gnousar sickness was upon the three travellers, and that their very mules were dripping with it, and suppose that they were driven to the city by hunger, but suggest no better reason for so terrible a crime.

But most believe that it was a message from the desert himself, who owns all the Earth to the southwards, spoken with his peculiar cry to those three who knew his voice—

men who had been out on the sand-wastes without tents by
night, who had been by day without water, men who had
been out there where the desert mutters, and had grown to
know his needs and his malevolence. They say that the
desert had a need for Bethmoora, that he wished to come
into her lovely streets, and to send into her temples and her
houses his storm-winds draped with sand. For he hates the
sound and the sight of men in his old evil heart, and he would
have Bethmoora silent and undisturbed, save for the weird
love he whispers at her gates.

If I knew what that message was that the three men
brought on mules, and told in the copper gate, I think that
I should go and see Bethmoora once again. For a great
longing comes on me here in London to see once more that
white and beautiful city; and yet I dare not, for I know not
the danger I should have to face, whether I should risk the
fury of unknown dreadful gods, or some disease unspeakable
and slow, or the desert's curse, or torture in some little pri-
vate room of the Emperor Thuba Mleen, or something that
the travellers have not told—perhaps more fearful still.

IDLE DAYS ON THE YANN

S O I came down through the wood to the bank of Yann
and found, as had been prophesied, the ship *Bird of the
River* about to loose her cable.

The captain sate cross-legged upon the white deck with his
scimitar lying beside him in its jewelled scabbard, and the
sailors toiled to spread the nimble sails to bring the ship into
the central stream of Yann, and all the while sang ancient
soothing songs. And the wind of the evening descending
cool from the snowfields of some mountainous abode of distant gods came suddenly, like glad tidings to an anxious city,
into the wing-like sails.

And so we came into the central stream, whereat the sailors lowered the greater sails. But I had gone to bow before
the captain, and to inquire concerning the miracles, and ap-
pearances among men, of the most holy gods of whatever
land he had come from. And the captain answered that he
came from fair Belzoond, and worshipped gods that were
the least and humblest, who seldom sent the famine or the
thunder, and were easily appeased with little battles. And
I told how I came from Ireland, which is of Europe, whereat
the captain and all the sailors laughed, for they said, "There
are no such places in all the land of dreams." When they
had ceased to mock me, I explained that my fancy mostly
dwelt in the desert of Cuppar-Nombo, about a beautiful blue
city called Golthoth the Damned, which was sentinelled all
round by wolves and their shadows, and had been utterly

desolate for years and years, because of a curse which the gods once spoke in anger and could never since recall. And sometimes my dreams took me as far as Pungar Vees, the red walled city where the fountains are, which trades with the Isles and Thul. When I said this they complimented me upon the abode of my fancy, saying that, though they had never seen these cities, such places might well be imagined. For the rest of that evening I bargained with the captain over the sum that I should pay him for my fare if God and the tide of Yann should bring us safely as far as the cliffs by the sea, which are named Bar-Wul-Yann, the Gate of Yann.

And now the sun had set, and all the colors of the world and heaven had held a festival with him, and slipped one by one away before the imminent approach of night. The parrots had all flown home to the jungle on either bank, the monkeys in rows in safety on high branches of the trees were silent and asleep, the fireflies in the deeps of the forest were going up and down, and the great stars came gleaming out to look on the face of Yann. Then the sailors lighted lanterns and hung them round the ship, and the light flashed out on a sudden and dazzled Yann, and the ducks that fed along his marshy banks all suddenly arose, and made wide circles in the upper air, and saw the distant reaches of the Yann and the white mist that softly cloaked the jungle, before they returned again into their marshes.

And then the sailors knelt on the decks and prayed, not all together, but five or six at a time. Side by side there kneeled down together five or six, for there only prayed at the same time men of different faiths, so that no god should hear two men praying to him at once. As soon as any one had finished his prayer, another of the same faith would take his place. Thus knelt the row of five or six with bended heads under the fluttering sail, while the central stream of the River Yann took them on towards the sea and their prayers rose up from among the lanterns and went towards the stars. And behind them in the after end of the ship the helmsman prayed aloud the helmsman's prayer, which is prayed by all who follow his trade upon the River Yann, of whatever faith they be. And the captain prayed to his little lesser gods, to the gods that bless Belzoond.

And I, too, felt that I would pray. Yet I liked not to pray to a jealous God there where the frail affectionate gods whom the heathen love were being humbly invoked; so I bethought me, instead, of Sheol Nugganoth, whom the men of the jungle have long since deserted, who is now unworshipped and alone; and to him I prayed.

And upon us praying the night came suddenly down, as it comes upon all men who pray at evening and upon all men who do not; yet our prayers comforted our own souls when we thought of the Great Night to come.

And so Yann bore us magnificently onwards, for he was elate with molten snow that the Poltiades had brought him from the Hills of Hap; and the Marn and Migris were swollen full with floods; and he bore us in his might past Kyph and Pir, and we saw the lights of Goolunza.

Soon we all slept except the helmsman, who kept the ship in the mid-stream of Yann.

When the sun rose the helmsman ceased to sing, for by song he cheered himself in the lonely night. When the song ceased we suddenly all awoke, and another took the helm, and the helmsman slept.

We know that soon we should come to Mandaroon. We made a meal, and Mandaroon appeared. Then the captain commanded, and the sailors loosed again the greater sails, and the ship turned and left the stream of Yann and came into a harbour beneath the ruddy walls of Mandaroon. Then while the sailors went and gathered fruits I came alone to the gate of Mandaroon. A few huts were outside it, in which lived the guard. A sentinel with a long white beard was standing in the gate, armed with a rusty pike. He wore large spectacles, which were covered with dust. Through the gate I saw the city. A deathly stillness was over all of it. The ways seemed untrodden, and moss was thick on door-steps; in the market-place huddled figures lay asleep. A scent of incense came wafted through the gateway, of incense and burned poppies, and there was a hum of the echoes of distant bells. I said to the sentinel in the tongue of the region of Yann, "Why are they all asleep in this still city?"

He answered: "None may ask questions in this gate for fear they wake the people of the city. For when the people of this city wake the gods will die. And when the gods die men may dream no more." And I began to ask him what gods that city worshipped, but he lifted his pike because none might ask questions there. So I left him and went back to the *Bird of the River*.

Certainly Mandaroon was beautiful with her white pinnacles peering over her ruddy walls and the green of her copper roofs.

When I came back again to the *Bird of the River,* I found the sailors were returned to the ship. Soon we weighed anchor, and sailed out again, and so came once more to the middle of the river. And now the sun was moving toward his heights, and there had reached us on the River Yann the song of those countless myriads of choirs that attend him in his progress round the world. For the little creatures that have many legs had spread their gauze wings easily on the air, as a man rests his elbows on a balcony and gave jubilant, ceremonial praises to the sun, or else they moved together on the air in wavering dances intricate and swift, or turned aside to avoid the onrush of some drop of water that a breeze had shaken from a jungle orchid, chilling the air and driving it before it, as it fell whirring in its rush to the earth; but all the while they sang triumphantly. "For the day is for us," they said, "whether our great and sacred father the Sun shall bring up more like us from the marshes, or whether all the world shall end to-night." And there sang all those whose notes are known to human ears, as well as those whose far more numerous notes have been never heard by man.

To these a rainy day had been as an era of war that should desolate continents during all the lifetime of a man.

And there came out also from the dark and steaming jungle to behold and rejoice in the Sun the huge and lazy butterflies. And they danced, but danced idly, on the ways of the air, as some haughty queen of distant conquered lands might in her poverty and exile dance, in some encampment of the gipsies, for the mere bread to live by, but beyond that would never abate her pride to dance for a fragment more.

And the butterflies sung of strange and painted things, of purple orchids and of lost pink cities and the monstrous colours of the jungle's decay. And they, too, were among those whose voices are not discernible by human ears. And as they floated above the river, going from forest to forest, their splendour was matched by the inimical beauty of the birds who darted out to pursue them. Or sometimes they settled on the white and wax-like blooms of the plant that creeps and clambers about the trees of the forest; and their purple wings flashed out on the great blossoms as, when the caravans go from Nurl to Thace, the gleaming silks flash out upon the snow, where the crafty merchants spread them one by one to astonish the mountaineers of the Hills of Noor.

But upon men and beasts the sun sent a drowsiness. The river monsters along the river's marge lay dormant in the slime. The sailors pitched a pavillion, with golden tassels, for the captain upon the deck, and then went, all but the helmsman, under a sail that they had hung as an awning between two masts. Then they told tales to one another, each of his own city or of the miracles of his god, until all were fallen asleep. The captain offered me the shade of his pavillion with the gold tassels, and there we talked for awhile, he telling me that he was taking merchandise to Perdondaris, and that he would take back to fair Belzoond things appertaining to the affairs of the sea. Then, as I watched through the pavillion's opening the brilliant birds and butterflies that crossed and re-crossed over the river, I fell asleep, and dreamed that I was a monarch entering his capital underneath arches of flags, and all the musicians of the world were there, playing melodiously their instruments; but no one cheered.

In the afternoon, as the day grew cooler again, I awoke and found the captain buckling on his scimitar, which he had taken off him while he rested.

And now we were approaching the wide court of Astahahn, which opens upon the river. Strange boats of antique design were chained there to the steps. As we neared it we saw the open marble court, on three sides of which stood the city fronting on colonnades. And in the court and along the colonnades the people of that city walked with solemnity and care according to the rites of ancient ceremony. All in that city was of ancient device; the carving on the houses, which, when age had broken it, remained unrepaired, was of the remotest times, and everywhere were represented in stone beasts that have long since passed away from Earth—the dragon, the griffin, and the hippogriffin, and the different species of gargoyle. Nothing was to be found, whether material or custom, that was new in Astahahn. Now they took no notice at all of us as we went by, but continued their processions and ceremonies in the ancient city, and the sailors, knowing their custom, took no notice of them. But I called, as we came near, to one who stood beside the water's edge, asking him what men did in Astahahn and what their merchandise was, and with whom they traded. He said, "Here we have fettered and manacled Time, who would otherwise slay the gods."

I asked him what gods they worshipped in that city, and he said, "All those gods whom Time has not yet slain." Then he turned from me and would say no more, but busied himself in behaving in accordance with ancient custom. And so, according to the will of Yann, we drifted onwards and left Astahahn. The river widened below Astahahn, and we found in greater quantities such birds as prey on fishes. And they were very wonderful in their plumage, and they came not out of the jungle, but flew, with their long necks stretched out before them, and their legs lying on the wind behind, straight up the river over the mid-stream.

And now the evening began to gather in. A thick white mist had appeared over the river, and was softly rising higher. It clutched at the trees with long impalpable arms, it rose higher and higher, chilling the air; and white shapes moved away into the jungle as though the ghosts of shipwrecked mariners were searching stealthily in the darkness for the spirits of evil that long ago had wrecked them on the Yann. As the sun sank behind the field of orchids that grew on the matted summit of the jungle, the river monsters came wallowing out of the slime in which they had reclined during the heat of the day, and the great beasts of the jungle came down to drink. The butterflies a while since were gone to rest. In little narrow tributaries that we passed night seemed already to have fallen, though the sun which had disappeared from us had not yet set.

And now the birds of the jungle came flying home far over us, with the sunlight glistening pink upon their breasts, and lowered their pinions as soon as they saw the Yann, and dropped into the trees. And the widgeon began to go up the river in great companies, all whistling, and then would suddenly wheel and all go down again. And there shot by us the small and arrow-like teal; and we heard the manifold cries of flocks of geese, which the sailors told me had recently come in from crossing over the Lispasian ranges; every year they come by the same way, close by the peak of Mluna, leaving it to the left, and the mountain eagles know the way they come and—men say—the very hour, and every year they expect them by the same way as soon as the snows have fallen upon the Northern Plains. But soon it grew so dark that we saw these birds no more, and only heard the whirring of their wings, and of countless others besides, until they all

settled down along the banks of the river, and it was the
hour when the birds of the night went forth. Then the sailors lit the lanterns for the night, and huge moths appeared,
flapping about the ship, and at moments their gorgeous colours would be revealed by the lanterns, then they would pass
into the night again, where all was black. And again the
sailors prayed, and thereafter we supped and slept, and the
helmsman took our lives into his care.

When I awoke I found that we had indeed come to Perdóndaris, that famous city. For there it stood upon the left
of us, a city fair and notable, and all the more pleasant for
our eyes to see after the jungle that was so long with us.
And we were anchored by the market-place, and the captain's
merchandise was all displayed, and a merchant of Perdóndaris stood looking at it. And the captain had his scimitar
in his hand, and was beating with it in anger upon the deck,
and the splinters were flying up from the white planks; for
the merchant had offered him a price for his merchandise
that the captain declared to be an insult to himself and his
country's gods, whom he now said to be great and terrible
gods, whose curses were to be dreaded. But the merchant
waved his hands, which were of great fatness, showing the
pink palms, and swore that of himself he thought not at all,
but only of the poor folk in the huts beyond the city to whom
he wished to sell the merchandise for as low a price as pos-
sible, leaving no remuneration for himself. For the merchandise was mostly the thick toomarund carpets that in the
winter keep the wind from the floor, and tollub which the
people smoke in pipes. Therefore the merchant said if he
offered a piffek more the poor folk must go without their
toomarunds when the winter came, and without their tollub
in the evenings, or else he and his aged father must starve
together. Thereat the captain lifted his scimitar to his own
throat, saying that he was now a ruined man, and that nothing remained to him but death. And while he was carefully
lifting his beard with his left hand, the merchant eyed the

merchandise again, and said that rather than see so worthy
a captain die, a man for whom he had conceived an especial
love when first he saw the manner in which he handled his
ship, he and his aged father should starve together and therefore he offered fifteen piffeks more.

When he said this the captain prostrated himself and
prayed to his gods that they might yet sweeten this merchant's bitter heart—to his little lesser gods, to the gods that
bless Belzoond.

At last the merchant offered yet five piffeks more. Then
the captain wept, for he said that he was deserted of his
gods; and the merchant also wept, for he said that he was
thinking of his aged father, and of how he soon would starve,
and he hid his weeping face with both his hands, and eyed
the tollub again between his fingers, And so the bargain was
concluded, and the merchant took the toomarund and tollub,
paying for them out of a great clinking purse. And these
were packed up into bales again, and three of the merchant's
slaves carried them upon their heads into the city. And all
the while the sailors had sat silent, cross-legged in a crescent
upon the deck, eagerly watching the bargain, and now a murmur of satisfaction arose among them, and they began to
compare it among themselves with other bargains that they
had known. And I found out from them that there are seven
merchants in Perdóndaris, and that they had all come to the
captain one by one before the bargaining began, and each
had warned him privately against the others. And to all the
merchants the captain had offered the wine of his own country, that they make in fair Belzoond, but could in no wise
persuade them to it. But now that the bargain was over,
and the sailors were seated at the first meal of the day, the
captain appeared among them with a cask of that wine, and
we broached it with care and all made merry together. And
the captain was glad in his heart because he knew that he had
much honour in the eyes of his men because of the bargain
that he had made. So the sailors drank the **wine of** their

native land, and soon their thoughts were back in fair Belzoond and the little neighbouring cities of Durl and Duz.

But for me the captain poured into a little glass some heavy yellow wine from a small jar which he kept apart among his sacred things. Thick and sweet it was, even like honey, yet there was in its heart a mighty, ardent fire which had authority over souls of men. It was made, the captain told me, with great subtlety by the secret craft of a family of six who lived in a hut on the mountains of Hian Min. Once in these mountains, he said, he followed the spoor of a bear, and he came suddenly on a man of that family who had hunted the same bear, and he was at the end of a narrow way with precipice all about him, and his spear was sticking in the bear, and the wound not fatal, and he had no other weapon. And the bear was walking towards the man, very slowly because his wound irked him—yet he was now very close. And what the captain did he would not say, but every year as soon as the snows are hard, and travelling is easy on the Hian Min, that man comes down to the market in the plains, and always leaves for the captain in the gate of fair Belzoond a vessel of that priceless secret wine.

And as I sipped the wine and the captain talked, I remembered me of stalwart noble things that I had long since resolutely planned, and my soul seemed to grow mightier within me and to dominate the whole tide of the Yann. It may be that I then slept. Or, if I did not, I do not now minutely recollect every detail of that morning's occupations. Towards evening, I awoke and wishing to see Perdóndaris before we left in the morning, and being unable to wake the captain, I went ashore alone. Certainly Perdóndaris was a powerful city; it was encompassed by a wall of great strength and altitude, having in it hollow ways for troops to walk in, and battlements along it all the way, and fifteen strong towers on it in every mile, and copper plaques low down where men could read them, telling in all the languages of those parts of the Earth—one language on each plaque—the tale of how

an army once attacked Perdóndaris and what befel that army.
Then I entered Perdóndaris and found all the people dancing,
clad in brilliant silks, and playing on the tambang as they
danced. For a fearful thunderstorm had terrified them while
I slept, and the fires of death, they said, had danced over
Perdóndaris, and now the thunder had gone leaping away
large and black and hideous, they said, over the distant hills,
and had turned round snarling at them, showing his gleaming
teeth, and had stamped, as he went, upon the hilltops until
they rang as though they had been bronze. And often and
again they stopped in their merry dances and prayed to the
God they knew not, saying, "O, God that we know not, we
thank Thee for sending the thunder back to his hills." And I
went on and came to the market-place, and lying there upon
the marble pavement I saw the merchant fast asleep and
breathing heavily, with his face and the palms of his hands
towards the sky, and slaves were fanning him to keep away
the flies. And from the market-place I came to a silver
temple and then to a palace of onyx, and there were many
wonders in Perdóndaris, and I would have stayed and seen
them all, but as I came to the outer wall of the city I suddenly saw in it a huge ivory gate. For a while I paused
and admired it, then I came nearer and perceived the dreadful truth. The gate was carved out of one solid piece!

I fled at once through the gateway and down to the ship,
and even as I ran I thought that I heard far off on the hills
behind me the tramp of the fearful beast by whom that mass
of ivory was shed, who was perhaps even then looking for
his other tusk. When I was on the ship again I felt safer,
and I said nothing to the sailors of what I had seen.

And now the captain was gradually awakening. Now night
was rolling up from the East and North, and only the pinnacles of the towers of Perdóndaris still took the fallen sunlight. Then I went to the captain and told him quietly of
the thing I had seen. And he questioned me at once about
the gate, in a low voice, that the sailors might not know; and

I told him how the weight of the thing was such that it could not have been brought from afar, and the captain knew that it had not been there a year ago. We agreed that such a beast could never have been killed by any assault of man, and then the gate must have been a fallen tusk, and one fallen near and recently. Therefore he decided that it were better to flee at once; so he commanded, and the sailors went to the sails, and others raised the anchor to the deck, and just as the highest pinnacle of marble lost the last rays of the sun we left Perdóndaris, that famous city. And night came down and cloaked Perdóndaris and hid it from our eyes, which as things have happened will never see it again; for I have heard since that something swift and wonderful has suddenly wrecked Perdóndaris in a day—towers and walls, and people.

And the night deepened over the River Yann, a night all white with stars. And with the night there rose the helmsman's song. As soon as he had prayed he began to sing to cheer himself all through the lonely night. But first he prayed, praying the helmsman's prayer. And this is what I remember of it, rendered into English with a very feeble equivalent of the rhythm that seemed so resonant in those tropic nights.

To whatever god may hear.

Wherever there be sailors whether of river or sea: whether their way be dark or whether through storm: whether their peril be of beast or of rock: or from enemy lurking on land or pursuing on sea: wherever the tiller is cold or the helmsman stiff: wherever sailors sleep or helmsmen watch: guard, guide, and return us to the old land, that has known us: to the far homes that we know.

> To all the gods that are.
> To whatever god may hear.

So he prayed, and there was silence. And the sailors laid them down to rest for the night. The silence deepened, and was only broken by the ripples of Yann that lightly touched our prow. Sometimes some monster of the river coughed.

Silence and ripples, ripples and silence again.

And then his loneliness came upon the helmsman, and he began to sing. And he sang the market songs of Durl and Duz, and the old dragon-legends of Belzoond.

Many a song he sang, telling to spacious and exotic Yann the little tales and trifles of his city of Durl. And the songs welled up over the black jungle and came into the clear cold air above, and the great bands of stars that look on Yann began to know the affairs of Durl and Duz, and of the shepherds that dwelt in the fields between, and the flocks that they had, and the loves that they had loved, and all the little things that they hoped to do. And as I lay wrapped up in skins and blankets, listening to those songs, and watching the fantastic shapes of the great trees like to black giants stalking through the night, I suddenly fell asleep.

When I awoke great mists were trailing away from the Yann. And the flow of the river was tumbling now tumultuously, and little waves appeared; for Yann had scented from afar the ancient crags of Glorm, and knew that their ravines lay cool before him wherein he should meet the merry wild Irillion rejoicing from fields of snow. So he shook off from him the torpid sleep that had come upon him in the hot and scented jungle, and forgot its orchids and its butterflies, and swept on turbulent, expectant, strong; and soon the snowy peaks of the Hills of Glorm came glittering into view. And now the sailors were waking up from sleep. Soon we all eat. and then the helmsman laid him down to sleep while a comrade took his place, and they all spread over him their choicest furs.

And in a while we heard the sound that the Irillion made as she came down dancing from the fields of snow.

And then we saw the ravine in the Hills of Glorm lying precipitous and smooth before us, into which we were carried by the leaps of Yann. And now we left the steamy jungle and breathed the mountain air; the sailors stood up and took deep breaths of it, and thought of their own far-off Acroctian hills on which were Durl and Duz—below them in the plains stands fair Belzoond.

A great shadow brooded between the cliffs of Glorm, but the crags were shining above us like gnarled moons, and almost lit the gloom. Louder and louder came the Irillion's song, and the sound of her dancing down from the fields of snow. And soon we saw her white and full of mists, and wreathed with rainbows delicate and small that she had plucked up near the mountain's summit from some celestial garden of the Sun. Then she went away seawards with the huge grey Yann and the ravine widened, and opened upon the world, and our rocking ship came through to the light of the day.

And all that morning and all the afternoon we passed through the marshes of Pondoovery; and Yann widened there, and flowed solemnly and slowly, and the captain bade the sailors beat on bells to overcome the dreariness of the marshes.

At last the Irusian mountains came in sight, nursing the villages of Pen-Kai and Blut, and the wandering streets of Mlo, where priests propitiate the avalanche with wine and maize. Then night came down over the plains of Tlun, and we saw the lights of Cappadarnia. We heard the Pathnites beating upon drums as we passed the Imaut and Golzunda, then all but the helmsman slept. And villages scattered along the banks of the Yann heard all that night in the helmsman's unknown tongue the little songs of cities that they knew not.

I awoke before dawn with a feeling that I was unhappy before I remembered why. Then I recalled that by the evening of the approaching day, according to all foreseen probabilities, we should come to Bar-Wul-Yann, and I should part from the captain and his sailors. And I had liked the man because he had given me of his yellow wine that was set apart

among his sacred things, and many a story he had told me
about his fair Belzoond between the Acroctian hills and the
Hian Min. And I had liked the ways that his sailors had,
and the prayers that they prayed at evening side by side,
grudging not one another their alien gods. And I had a
liking too for the tender way in which they often spoke of
Durl and Duz, for it is good that men should love their native cities and the little hills that hold those cities up.

And I had come to know who would meet them when
they returned to their homes, and where they thought the
meetings would take place, some in a valley of the Acroctian
hills where the road comes up from Yann, others in the gateway of one or another of the three cities, and others by the
fireside in the home. And I thought of the danger that had
menaced us all alike outside Perdóndaris, a danger that, as
things have happened, was very real.

And I thought too of the helmsman's cheery song in the
cold and lonely night, and how he had held our lives in his
careful hands. And as I thought of this the helmsman ceased
to sing, and I looked up and saw a pale light had appeared
in the sky, and the lonely night had passed; and the dawn
widened, and the sailors awoke.

And soon we saw the tide of the Sea himself advancing
resolute between Yann's borders, and Yann sprang lithely at
him and they struggled awhile; then Yann and all that was
his were pushed back northward, so that the sailors had to
hoist the sails and, the wind being favorable, we still held
onwards.

And we passed Góndara and Narl and Haz. And we saw
memorable, holy Golnuz, and heard the pilgrims praying.

When we awoke after the midday rest we were coming
near to Nen, the last of the cities on the River Yann. And
the jungle was all about us once again, and about Nen;
but the great Mloon ranges stood up over all things, and
watched the city from beyond the jungle.

Here we anchored, and the captain and I went up into

the city and found that the Wanderers had come into Nen.

And the Wanderers were a weird, dark tribe, that once in every seven years came down from the peaks of Mloon, having crossed by a pass that is known to them from some fantastic land that lies beyond. And the people of Nen were all ɔutside their houses, and all stood wondering at their own streets. For the men and women of the Wanderers had crowded all the ways, and every one was doing some strange thing. Some danced astounding dances that they had learned from the desert wind, rapidly curving and swirling till the eye could follow no longer. Others played upon instruments beautiful wailing tunes that were full of horror, which souls had taught them lost by night in the desert, that strange far desert from which the Wanderers came.

None of their instruments were such as were known in Nen nor in any part of the region of the Yann; even the horns out of which some were made were of beasts that none had seen along the river, for they were barbed at the tips. And they sang, in the language of none, songs that seemed to be akin to the mysteries of night and to the unreasoned fear that haunts dark places.

Bitterly all the dogs of Nen distrusted them. And the Wanderers told one another fearful tales, for though no one in Nen knew ought of their language yet they could see the fear on the listeners' faces, and as the tale wound on the whites of their eyes showed vividly in terror as the eyes of some little beast whom the hawk has seized. Then the teller of the tale would smile and stop, and another would tell his story, and the teller of the first tale's lips would chatter with fear. And if some deadly snake chanced to appear the Wanderers would greet him as a brother, and the snake would seem to give his greetings to them before he passed on again. Once that most fierce and lethal of tropic snakes, the giant lythra, came out of the jungle and all down the street, the central street of Nen, and none of the Wanderers moved away from him, but they all played sonorously on drums, as though he had been a person of much honour; and the snake moved through the midst of them and smote none.

Even the Wanderers' children could do strange things, for if any one of them met with a child of Nen the two would stare at each other in silence with large grave eyes; then the Wanderers' child would slowly draw from his turban a live fish or snake. And the children of Nen could do nothing of that kind at all.

Much I should have wished to stay and hear the hymn with which they greet the night, that is answered by the wolves on the heights of Mloon, but it was now time to raise the anchor again that the captain might return from Bar-Wul-Yann upon the landward tide. So we went on board and continued down the Yann. And the captain and I spoke little, for we were thinking of our parting, which should be for long, and we watched instead the splendour of the westerning sun. For the sun was a ruddy gold, but a faint mist cloaked the jungle, lying low, and into it poured the smoke of the little jungle cities, and the smoke of them met together in the mist and joined into one haze, which became purple, and was lit by the sun, as the thoughts of men become hallowed by some great and sacred thing. Some times one column from a lonely house would rise up higher than the cities' smoke, and gleam by itself in the sun.

And now as the sun's last rays were nearly level, we saw the sight that I had come to see, for from two mountains that stood on either shore two cliffs of pink marble came out into the river, all glowing in the light of the low sun, and they were quite smooth and of mountainous altitude, and they nearly met, and Yann went tumbling between them and found the sea.

And this was Bar-Wul-Yann, the Gate of Yann, and in the distance through that barrier's gap I saw the azure indescribable sea, where little fishing-boats went gleaming by.

And the sun set, and the brief twilight came, and the exultation of the glory of Bar-Wul-Yann was gone, yet still the

pink cliffs glowed, the fairest marvel that the eye beheld—
and this in a land of wonders. And soon the twilight gav
place to the coming out of stars, and the colours of Bar-Wul
Yann went dwindling away. And the sight of those cliff
was to me as some chord of music that a master's hand had
launched from the violin, and which carries to Heaven o
Faëry the tremulous spirits of men.

And now by the shore they anchored and went no further
for they were sailors of the river and not of the sea, and knew
the Yann but not the tides beyond.

And the time was come when the captain and I must part
he to go back again to his fair Belzoond in sight of the distant peaks of the Hian Min, and I to find my way by strange
means back to those hazy fields that all poets know, wherein
stand small mysterious cottages through whose windows, looking westwards, you may see the fields of men, and looking
eastwards see glittering elfin mountains, tipped with snow
going range on range into the region of Myth, and beyond
it into the kingdom of Fantasy, which pertain to the Lands
of Dream. Long we regarded one another, knowing that
we should meet no more, for my fancy is weakening as the
years slip by, and I go ever more seldom into the Lands of
Dream. Then we clasped hands, uncouthly on his part, for
it is not the method of greeting in his country, and he commended my soul to the care of his own gods, to his little
lesser gods, the humble ones, to the gods that bless Belzoond.

THE SWORD AND THE IDOL

I T was a cold winter's evening late in the Stone Age; the
sun had gone down blazing over the plains of Thold;
there were no clouds, only the chill blue sky and the im-
minence of stars; and the surface of the sleeping Earth began
to harden against the cold of the night. Presently from their
lairs arose, and shook themselves and went stealthily forth,
those of Earth's children to whom it is the law to prowl
abroad as soon as the dusk has fallen. And they went pattering softly over the plain, and their eyes shone in the dark,
and crossed and recrossed one another in their courses. Suddenly there became manifest in the midst of the plain that
fearful portent of the presence of Man—a little flickering
fire. And the children of Earth who prowl abroad by night
looked sideways at it and snarled and edged away; all but
the wolves, who came a little nearer, for it was winter and
the wolves were hungry, and they had come in thousands
from the mountains, and they said in their hearts, "We are
strong." Around the fire a little tribe was encamped. They,
too, had come from the mountains, and from lands beyond
them, but it was in the mountains that the wolves first winded
them; they picked up bones at first that the tribe had
dropped, but they were closer now and on all sides. It was
Loz who had lit the fire. He had killed a small furry beast,
hurling his stone axe at it, and had gathered a quantity of
reddish brown stones, and had laid them in a long row, and

placed bits of the small beast all along it; then he lit a fire on each side, and the stones heated, and the bits began to cook. It was at this time that the tribe noticed that the wolves who had followed them so far were no longer content with the scraps of deserted encampments. A line of yellow eyes surrounded them, and when it moved it was to come nearer. So the men of the tribe hastily tore up brushwood, and felled a small tree with their flint axes, and heaped it all over the fire that Loz had made, and for a while the great heap hid the flame, and the wolves came trotting in and sat down again on their haunches much closer than before; and the fierce and valiant dogs that belonged to the tribe believed that their end was about to come while fighting, as they had long since prophesied it would. Then the flame caught the lofty stack of brushwood, and rushed out of it, and ran up the side of it, and stood up haughtily far over the top, and the wolves seeing this terrible ally of Man revelling there in his strength, and knowing nothing of his frequent treachery to his masters, went slowly away as though they had other purposes. And for the rest of that night the dogs of the encampment cried out to them and besought them to come back. But the tribe lay down all round the fire under thick furs and slept. And a great wind arose and blew into the roaring heart of the fire till it was red no longer, but all pallid with heat. With the dawn the tribe awoke.

Loz might have known that after such a mighty conflagration nothing could remain of his small furry beast, but there was hunger in him and little reason as he searched among the ashes. What he found there amazed him beyond measure; there was no meat, there was not even his row of reddish brown stones, but something longer than a man's leg and narrower than his hand, was lying there like a great flattened snake. When Loz looked at its thin edges and saw that it ran to a point, he picked up stones to chip it and make it sharp. It was the instinct of Loz to sharpen things. When he found that it could not be chipped his wonderment increased. It was many hours before he discovered that he could sharpen the edges by rubbing them with a stone; but at last the point was sharp, and all one side of it except near the end, where Loz held it in his hand. And Loz lifted it and brandished it, and the Stone Age was over. That afternoon in the little encampment, just as the tribe moved on, the Stone Age passed away, which, for perhaps thirty or forty thousand years, had slowly lifted Man from among the beasts and left him with his supremacy beyond all hope of reconquest.

It was not for many days that any other man tried to make for himself an iron sword by cooking the same kind of small furry beast that Loz had tried to cook. It was not for many years that any thought to lay the meat along stones as Loz had done; and when they did, being no longer on the plains of Thold, they used flints or chalk. It was not for many generations that another piece of iron ore was melted and the secret slowly guessed. Nevertheless one of Earth's many veils was torn aside by Loz to give us ultimately the steel sword and the plough, machinery and factories; let us not blame Loz if we think that he did wrong, for he did all in ignorance. The tribe moved on until it came to water, and there it settled down under a hill, and they built their huts there. Very soon they had to fight with another tribe, a tribe that was stronger than they; but the sword of Loz was terrible and his tribe slew their foes. You might make one blow at Loz, but then would come one thrust from that iron sword, and there was no way of surviving it. No one could fight with Loz. And he became the ruler of the tribe in the place of Iz, who hitherto had ruled it with his sharp axe, as his father had before him.

Now Loz begat Lo, and in his old age gave his sword to him, and Lo ruled the tribe with it. And Lo called the name of the sword Death, because it was so swift and terrible.

And Iz begat Ird, who was of no account. And Ird hated

Lo because he was of no account by reason of the iron sword of Lo.

One night Ird stole down to the hut of Lo, carrying his sharp axe, and he went very softly, but Lo's dog, Warner, heard him coming, and he growled softly by his master's door. When Ird came to the hut he heard Lo talking gently to his sword. And Lo was saying, "Lie still, Death. Rest, rest, old sword," and then, "What, again, Death? Be still. Be still."

And then again: "What, art thou hungry, Death? Or thirsty, poor old sword? Soon, Death, soon. Be still only a little."

But Ird fled, for he did not like the gentle tone of Lo as he spoke to his sword.

And Lo begat Lod. And when Lo died Lod took the iron sword and ruled the tribe.

And Ird begat Ith, who was of no account, like his father.

Now when Lod had smitten a man or killed a terrible beast, Ith would go away for a while into the forest rather than hear the praises that would be given to Lod.

And once, as Ith sat in the forest waiting for the day to pass, he suddenly thought he saw a tree trunk looking at him as with a face. And Ith was afraid, for trees should not look at men. But soon Ith saw that it was only a tree and not a man, though it was like a man. Ith used to speak to this tree, and tell it about Lod, for he dared not speak to any one else about him. And Ith found comfort in talking about Lod.

One day Ith went with his stone axe into the forest, and stayed there many days.

He came back by night, and the next morning when the tribe awoke they saw something that was like a man and yet was not a man. And it sat on the hill with its elbows pointing outwards and was quite still. And Ith was crouching before it, and hurriedly placing before it fruits and flesh, and then leaping away from it and looking frightened. Pres-

ently all the tribe came out to see, but dared not come quite
close because of the fear that they saw on the face of Ith.
And Ith went to his hut, and came back again with a hunting spear-head and valuable small stone knives, and reached
out and laid them before the thing that was like a man, and
then sprang away from it.

And some of the tribe questioned Ith about the still thing
that was like a man, and Ith said, "This is Ged." They then
asked, "Who is Ged?" and Ith said, "Ged sends the crops
and the rain; and the sun and the moon are Ged's."

Then the tribe went back to their huts, but later in the
day some came again, and they said to Ith, "Ged is only
as we are, having hands and feet." And Ith pointed to the
right hand of Ged, which was not as his left, but was shaped
like the paw of a beast, and Ith said, "By this ye may know
that he is not as any man."

Then they said, "He is indeed Ged." But Lod said, "He
speaketh not, nor doth he eat," and Ith answered, "The
thunder is his voice and the famine is his eating."

After this the tribe copied Ith, and brought little gifts of
meat to Ged; and Ith cooked them before him that Ged
might smell the cooking.

One day a great thunderstorm came trampling up from
the distance and raged among the hills, and the tribe all hid
away from it in their huts. And Ith appeared among the
huts looking unafraid. And Ith said little, but the tribe
thought that he had expected the terrible storm because the
meat that they had laid before Ged had been tough meat, and
not the best parts of the beasts they slew.

And Ged grew to have more honour among the tribe than
Lod. And Lod was vexed.

One night Lod arose when all were asleep, and quieted his
dog, and took his iron sword and went away to the hill. And
he came on Ged in the starlight, sitting still, with his elbows
pointing outwards, and his beast's paw, and the mark of
the fire on the ground where his food had been cooked.

And Lod stood there for a while in great fear, trying to keep to his purpose. Suddenly he stepped up close to Ged and lifted his iron sword, and Ged neither hit nor shrank. Then the thought came into Lod's mind, "Ged does not hit. What will Ged do instead?"

And Lod lowered his sword and struck not, and his imagination began to work on that, "What will Ged do instead?"

And the more Lod thought, the worse was his fear of Ged.

And Lod ran away and left him.

Lod still ruled the tribe in battle or in the hunt, but the chiefest spoils of battle were given to Ged, and the beasts that they slew were Ged's; and all questions that concerned war or peace, and questions of law and disputes, were always brought to him, and Ith gave the answers after speaking to Ged by night.

At last Ith said, the day after an eclipse, that the gifts which they brought to Ged were not enough, that some far greater sacrifice was needed, that Ged was very angry even now, and not to be appeased by any ordinary sacrifice.

And Ith said that to save the tribe from the anger of Ged he would speak to Ged that night, and ask him what new sacrifice he needed.

Deep in his heart Lod shuddered, for his instinct told him that Ged wanted Lod's only son, who should hold the iron sword when Lod was gone.

No one would dare touch Lod because of the iron sword, but his instinct said in his slow mind again and again, "Ged loves Ith. Ith has said so. Ith hates the sword-holders."

"Ith hates the sword-holders. Ged loves Ith."

Evening fell and the night came when Ith should speak with Ged, and Lod became even surer of the doom of his race.

He lay down but could not sleep.

Midnight had barely come when Lod arose and went with his iron sword again to the hill.

And there sat Ged. Had Ith been to him yet? Ith whom Ged loved, who hated the sword-holders.

And Lod looked long at the old sword of iron that had come to his grandfather on the plains of Thold.

Good-bye, old sword! And Lod laid it on the knees of Ged, then went away.

And when Ith came, a little before dawn, the sacrifice was found acceptable unto Ged.

THE IDLE CITY

THERE was once a city which was an idle city, wherein men told vain tales.

And it was that city's custom to tax all men that would enter in, with the toll of some idle story in the gate.

So all men paid to the watchers in the gate the toll of an idle story, and passed into the city unhindered and unhurt. And in a certain hour of the night when the king of that city arose and went pacing swiftly up and down the chamber of his sleeping, and called upon the name of the dead queen, then would the watchers fasten up the gate and go into that chamber to the king, and, sitting on the floor, would tell him all the tales that they had gathered. And listening to them some calmer mood would come upon the king, and listening still he would lie down again and at last fall asleep, and all the watchers silently would arise and steal away from the chamber.

A while ago wandering, I came to the gate of that city. And even as I came a man stood up to pay his toll to the watchers. They were seated cross-legged on the ground between him and the gate, and each one held a spear. Near him two other travellers sat on the warm sand waiting. And the man said:

"Now the city of Nombros forsook the worship of the gods and turned towards God. So the gods threw their cloaks over their faces and strode away from the city, and going into the haze among the hills passed through the

60

trunks of the olive groves into the sunset. But when they had already left the earth, they turned and looked through the gleaming folds of the twilight for the last time at their city; and they looked half in anger and half in regret, then turned and went away forever. But they sent back a Death, who bore a scythe, saying to it: "Slay half in the city that forsook us, but half of them spare alive that they may yet remember their old forsaken gods."

But God sent a destroying angel to show that He was God, saying unto him: "Go down and show the strength of mine arm unto that city and slay half of the dwellers therein, yet spare a half of them that they may know that I am God."

And at once the destroying angel put his hand to his sword, and the sword came out of the scabbard with a deep breath, like to the breath that a broad woodman takes before his first blow at some giant oak. Thereat the angel pointed his arms downwards, and bending his head between them, fell forward from Heaven's edge, and the spring of his ankles shot him downwards with his wings furled behind him. So he went slanting earthward through the evening with his sword stretched out before him, and he was like a javelin that some hunter hath hurled that returneth again to the earth: but just before he touched it he lifted his head and spread his wings with the under feathers forward, and alighted by the bank of the broad Flavro that divides the city of Nombros. And down the bank of the Flavro he fluttered low, like to a hawk over a new-cut cornfield when the little creatures of the corn are shelterless, and at the same time down the other bank the Death from the gods went mowing.

At once they saw each other, and the angel glared at the Death, and the Death leered back at him, and the flames in the eyes of the angel illumined with a red glare the mist that lay in the hollows of the sockets of the Death. Suddenly they fell on one another, sword to scythe. And the angel captured the temples of the gods, and set up over them the sign of God, and the Death captured the temples of God, and led into them the ceremonies and sacrifices of the gods; and all the while the centuries slipped quietly by going down the Flavro seawards.

And now some worship God in the temple of the gods, and others worship the gods in the temple of God, and still the angel hath not returned again to the rejoicing choirs, and still the Death hath not gone back to die with the dead gods; but all through Nombros they fight up and down, and still on each side of the Flavro the city lives.

And the watchers in the gate said, "Enter in."

Then another traveller rose up, and said:

"Solemnly between Huhenwazi and Nitcrana the huge grey clouds came floating. And those great mountains, heavenly Huhenwazi, and Nitcrana, the king of peaks, greeted them, calling them brothers. And the clouds were glad of their greeting for they meet with companions seldom in the lonely heights of the sky.

"But the vapours of evening said unto the earth-mist, 'What are those shapes that dare to move above us and to go where Nitcrana is and Huhenwazi?'

"And the earth-mist said in answer unto the vapours of evening, 'It is only an earth-mist that has become mad and has left the warm and comfortable earth, and has in his madness thought that his place is with Huhenwazi and Nitcrana.'

" 'Once,' said the vapours of evening, 'there were clouds, but this was many and many a day ago, as our forefathers have said. Perhaps the mad one thinks he is the clouds.'

"Then spake the earth-worms from the warm deeps of the mud, saying 'O, earth-mist, thou art indeed the clouds, and there are no clouds but thou. And as for Huhenwazi and Nitcrana, I cannot see them, and therefore they are not high, and there are no mountains in the world but those that I cast up every morning out of the deeps of the mud.'

"And the earth-mist and the vapours of evening were glad at the voice of the earth-worms, and looking earthward believed what they had said.

"And indeed it is better to be as the earth-mist, and to keep close to the warm mud at night, and to hear the earth-worm's comfortable speech, and not to be a wanderer in the cheerless heights, but to leave the mountains alone with their desolate snow, to draw what comfort they can from their vast aspect over all the cities of men, and from the whispers that they hear at evening of unknown distant Gods."

And the watchers in the gate said, "Enter in."

Then a man stood up who came out of the west, and told a western tale. He said:

"There is a road in Rome that runs through an ancient temple that once the gods had loved; it runs along the top of a great wall, and the floor of the temple lies far down beneath it, of marble, pink and white.

"Upon the temple floor I counted to the number of thirteen hungry cats.

" 'Sometimes,' they said among themselves, 'it was the gods that lived here, sometimes it was men, and now it's cats. So let us enjoy the sun on the hot marble before another people comes.

"For it was at that hour of a warm afternoon when my fancy is able to hear the silent voices.

"And the fearful leanness of all those thirteen cats moved me to go into a neighbouring fish shop, and there to buy a quantity of fishes. Then I returned and threw them all over the railing at the top of the great wall, and they fell for thirty feet, and hit the sacred marble with a smack.

"Now, in any other town but Rome, or in the minds of any other cats, the sight of fishes falling out of heaven had surely excited wonder. They rose slowly, and all stretched themselves, then they came leisurely towards the fishes. 'It is only a miracle,' they said in their hearts."

And the watchers in the gate said, "Enter in."

Proudly and slowly, as they spoke, drew up to them a camel, whose rider sought for entrance to the city. His face shone with the sunset by which for long he had steered for the city's gate. Of him they demanded toll. Whereat he spoke to his camel, and the camel roared and kneeled, and the man descended from him. And the man unwrapped from many silks a box of divers metals wrought by the Japanese, and on the lid of it were figures of men who gazed from some shore at an isle of the Inland Sea. This he showed to the watchers, and when they had seen it, said, "It has seemed to me that these speak to each other thus:

"Behold now Oojni, the dear one of the sea, the little mother sea that hath no storms. She goeth out from Oojni singing a song, and she returneth singing over her sands. Little is Oojni in the lap of the sea, and scarce to be perceived by wondering ships. White sails have never wafted her legends afar, they are told not by bearded wanderers of the sea. Her fireside tales are known not to the North, the dragons of China have not heard of them, nor those that ride on elephants through Ind.

"Men tell the tales and the smoke ariseth upwards; the smoke departeth and the tales are told.

"Oojni is not a name among the nations, she is not known of where the merchants meet, she is not spoken of by alien lips.

"Indeed, but Oojni is little among the isles, yet is she loved by those that know her coasts and her inland places hidden from the sea.

"Without glory, without fame, and without wealth, Oojni is greatly loved by a little people, and by a few; yet not by few, for all her dead still love her, and oft by night come whispering through her woods. Who could forget Oojni even among the dead?

"For here in Oojni, wot you, are homes of men, and gardens, and golden temples of the gods, and sacred places inshore from the sea, and many murmurous woods. And there is a path that winds over the hills to go into mysterious holy lands where dance by night the spirits of the woods, or sing unseen in the sunlight; and no one goes into these holy lands, for who that love Oojni would rob her of her mysteries, and the curious aliens come not. Indeed, but we love Oojni though she is so little; she is the little mother of our race, and the kindly nurse of all seafaring birds.

"And behold, even now caressing her, the gentle fingers of the mother sea, whose dreams are afar with that old wanderer Ocean.

"And yet let us forget not Fuzi-Yama, for he stands manifest over clouds and sea, misty below, and vague and indistinct, but clear above for all the isles to watch. The ships make all their journeys in his sight, the nights and the days go by him like a wind, the summers and winters under him flicker and fade, the lives of men pass quietly here and hence, and Fuzi-Yama watches there—and knows."

And the watchers in the gate said "Enter in."

And I, too, would have told them a tale, very wonderful and very true; one that I had told in many cities, which as yet had no believers. But now the sun had set, and the brief twilight gone, and ghostly silences were rising from far and darkening hills. A stillness hung over that city's gate. And the great silence of the solemn night was more acceptable to the watchers in the gate than any sound of man. Therefore they beckoned to us, and motioned with their hands that we should pass untaxed into the city. And softly we went up over the sand, and between the high rock pillars of the gate, and a deep stillness settled among the watchers, and the stars over them twinkled undisturbed.

For how short a while man speaks, and withal how vainly. And for how long he is silent. Only the other day I met a king in Thebes, who had been silent already for four thousand years.

THE HASHISH MAN

I WAS at dinner in London the other day. The ladies had gone upstairs, and no one sat on my right; on my left there was a man I did not know, but he knew my name somehow, apparently, for he turned to me after a while, and said, "I read a story of yours about Bethmoora in a review."

Of course I remembered the tale. It was about a beautiful Oriental city that was suddenly deserted in a day—nobody quite knew why. I said, "Oh, yes," and slowly searched in my mind for some more fitting acknowledgement of the compliment that his memory had paid me.

I was greatly astonished when he said, "You were wrong about the gnousar sickness; it was not that at all."

I said, "Why! Have you been there?"

And he said, "Yes; I do it with hashish. I know Bethmoora well." And he took out of his pocket a small box full of some black stuff that looked like tar, but had a stranger smell. He warned me not to touch it with my finger, as the stain remained for days. "I got it from a gipsy," he said. "He had a lot of it, as it had killed his father." But I interrupted him, for I wanted to know for certain what it was that had made desolate that beautiful city, Bethmoora, and why they fled from it swiftly in a day. "Was it because of the Desert's curse?" I asked. And he said, "Partly it was the fury of the Desert and partly the advice of the Emperor Thuba Mleen, for that fearful beast is in some way connected with the Desert on his mother's side." And he

66

told me this strange story: "You remember the sailor with the black scar, who was there on the day that you described when the messengers came on mules to the gate of Beth-moora, and all the people fled. I met this man in a tavern, drinking rum, and he told me all about the flight from Beth-moora, but knew no more than you did what the message was, or who had sent it. However, he said he would see Bethmoora once more whenever he touched again at an eastern port, even if he had to face the Devil. He often said that he would face the Devil to find out the mystery of that message that emptied Bethmoora in a day. And in the end he had to face Thuba Mleen, whose weak ferocity he had not imagined. For one day the sailor told me he had found a ship, and I met him no more after that in the tavern drinking rum. It was about that time that I got the hashish from the gipsy, who had a quantity that he did not want. It takes one literally out of oneself. It is like wings. You swoop over distant countries and into other worlds. Once I found out the secret of the universe. I have forgotten what it was, but I know that the Creator does not take Creation seriously, for I remember that He sat in Space with all His work in front of Him and laughed. I have seen incredible things in fearful worlds. As it is your imagination that takes you there, so it is only by your imagination that you can get back. Once out in æther I met a battered, prowling spirit, that had belonged to a man whom drugs had killed a hundred years ago; and he led me to regions that I had never imagined; and we parted in anger beyond the Pleiades, and I could not imagine my way back. And I met a huge grey shape that was the Spirit of some great people, perhaps of a whole star, and I besought It to show me my way home, and It halted beside me like a sudden wind and pointed, and, speaking quite softly, asked me if I discerned a certain tiny light, and I saw a far star faintly, and then It said to me, 'That is the Solar System,' and strode tremendously on. And somehow I imagined my way back, and only just in time, for my body was already stiffening in a chair in my room; and the fire had gone out and everything was cold, and I had to move each finger one by one, and there were pins and needles in them, and dreadful pains in the nails, which began to thaw; and at last I could move one arm, and reached a bell, and for a long time no one came, because every one was in bed. But at last a man appeared, and they got a doctor; and *he* said that it was hashish poisoning, but it would have been all right if I hadn't met that battered, prowling spirit.

"I could tell you astounding things that I have seen, but you want to know who sent that message to Bethmoora. Well, it was Thuba Mleen. And this is how I know. I often went to the city after that day that you wrote of (I used to take hashish of an evening in my flat), and I always found it uninhabited. Sand had poured into it from the desert, and the streets were yellow and smooth, and through open, swinging doors the sand had drifted.

"One evening I had put the guard in front of the fire, and settled into a chair and eaten my hashish, and the first thing that I saw when I came to Bethmoora was the sailor with the black scar, strolling down the street, and making footprints in the yellow sand. And now I knew that I should see what secret power it was that kept Bethmoora uninhabited.

"I saw that there was anger in the Desert, for there were storm clouds heaving along the skyline, and I heard a muttering amongst the sand.

"The sailor strolled on down the street, looking into the empty houses as he went; sometimes he shouted and sometimes he sang, and sometimes he wrote his name on a marble wall. Then he sat down on a step and ate his dinner. After a while he grew tired of the city, and came back up the street. As he reached the gate of green copper three men on camels appeared.

"I could do nothing. I was only a consciousness, invisible,

wandering: my body was in Europe. The sailor fought well with his fists, but he was over-powered and bound with ropes, and led away through the Desert.

"I followed for as long as I could stay, and found that they were going by the way of the Desert round the Hills of Hap towards Utnar Véhi, and then I knew that the camel men belonged to Thuba Mleen.

"I work in an insurance office all day, and I hope you won't forget me if ever you want to insure—life, fire, or motor—but that's no part of my story. I was desperately anxious to get back to my flat, though it is not good to take hashish two days running; but I wanted to see what they would do to the poor fellow, for I had heard bad rumours about Thuba Mleen. When at last I got away I had a letter to write; then I rang for my servant, and told him that I must not be disturbed, though I left my door unlocked in case of accidents. After that I made up a good fire, and sat down and partook of the pot of dreams. I was going to the palace of Thuba Mleen.

"I was kept back longer than usual by noises in the street, but suddenly I was up above the town; the European countries rushed by beneath me, and there appeared the thin white palace spires of horrible Thuba Mleen. I found him presently at the end of a little narrow room. A curtain of red leather hung behind him, on which all the names of God, written in Yannish, were worked with a golden thread. Three windows were small and high. The Emperor seemed no more than about twenty, and looked small and weak. No smiles came on his nasty yellow face, though he tittered continually. As I looked from his low forehead to his quivering under lip, I became aware that there was some horror about him, though I was not able to perceive what it was. And then I saw it—the man never blinked; and though later on I watched those eyes for a blink, it never happened once.

"And then I followed the Emperor's rapt glance, and I saw the sailor lying on the floor, alive but hideously rent, and the royal torturers were at work all round him. They had torn long strips from him, but had not detached them, and they were torturing the ends of them far away from the sailor." The man that I met at dinner told me many things which I must omit. "The sailor was groaning softly, and every time he groaned Thuba Mleen tittered. I had no sense of smell, but I could hear and see, and I do not know which was the most revolting—the terrible condition of the sailor or the happy unblinking face of horrible Thuba Mleen.

"I wanted to go away, but the time was not yet come, and I had to stay where I was.

"Suddenly the Emperor's face began to twitch violently and his under lip quivered faster, and he whimpered with anger, and cried with a shrill voice, in Yannish, to the captain of his torturers that there was a spirit in the room. I feared not, for living men cannot lay hands on a spirit, but all the torturers were appalled at his anger, and stopped their work, for their hands trembled with fear. Then two men of the spear-guard slipped from the room, and each of them brought back presently a golden bowl, with knobs on it, full of hashish; and the bowls were large enough for heads to have floated in had they been filled with blood. And the two men fell to rapidly, each eating with two great spoons— there was enough in each spoonful to have given dreams to a hundred men. And there came upon them soon the hashish state, and their spirits hovered, preparing to go free, while I feared horribly, but ever and anon they fell back again to the bodies, recalled by some noise in the room. Still the men ate, but lazily now, and without ferocity. At last the great spoons dropped out of their hands, and their spirits rose and left them. I could not flee. And the spirits were more horrible than the men, because they were young men, and not yet wholly moulded to fit their fearful souls. Still the sailor groaned softly, evoking little titters from the Emperor Thuba Mleen. Then the two spirits rushed at me, and swept me thence as gusts of wind sweep butterflies, and away we went from that small, pale, heinous man. There was no escaping from these spirits' fierce insistence. The energy in my minute lump of the drug was overwhelmed by the huge spoonsful that these men had eaten with both hands. I was whirled over Arvle Woondery, and brought to the lands of Snith, and swept on still until I came to Kragua, and beyond this to those bleak lands that are nearly unknown to fancy. And we came at last to those ivory hills that are named the Mountains of Madness, and I tried to struggle against the spirits of that frightful Emperor's men, for I heard on the other side of the ivory hills the pittering of those beasts that prey on the mad, as they prowled up and down. It was no fault of mine that my little lump of hashish could not fight with their horrible spoonsful. . . ."

Some one was tugging at the hall-door bell. Presently a servant came and told our host that a policeman in the hall wished to speak to him at once. He apologised to us, and went outside, and we heard a man in heavy boots, who spoke in a low voice to him. My friend got up and walked over to the window, and opened it, and looked outside. "I should think it will be a fine night," he said. Then he jumped out. When we put our astonished heads out of the window to look for him, he was already out of sight.

POOR OLD BILL

O N an antique haunt of sailors, a tavern of the sea, the light of day was fading. For several evenings I had frequented this place, in the hope of hearing something from the sailors, as they sat over strange wines, about a rumour that had reached my ears of a certain fleet of galleons of old Spain still said to be afloat in the South Seas in some uncharted region.

In this I was again to be disappointed. Talk was low and seldom, and I was about to leave, when a sailor, wearing earrings of pure gold, lifted up his head from his wine, and looking straight before him at the wall, told his tale loudly:

(When later on a storm of rain arose and thundered on the tavern's leaded panes, he raised his voice without effort and spoke on still. The darker it got the clearer his wild eyes shone.)

"A ship with sails of the olden time was nearing fantastic isles. We had never seen such isles.

"We all hated the captain, and he hated us. He hated us all alike, there was no favouritism about him. And he never would talk a word with any of us, except sometimes in the evening when it was getting dark he would stop and look up and talk a bit to the men he had hanged at the yard-arm.

"We were a mutinous crew. But Captain was the only man that had pistols. He slept with one under his pillow and kept one close beside him. There was a nasty look about the isles. They were small and flat as though they had come up only recently from the sea, and they had no sand or rocks like honest isles, but green grass down to the water. And there were little cottages there whose looks we did not like. Their thatches came almost down to the ground, and were strangely turned up at the corners, and under the low eaves were queer, dark windows whose little leaded panes were too thick to see through. And no one, man or beast, was walking about, so that you could not know what kind of people lived there. But Captain knew. And he went ashore and into one of the cottages, and someone lit lights inside, and the little windows wore an evil look.

"It was quite dark when he came aboard again, and he bade a cheery good-night to the men that swung from the yard-arm, and he eyed us in a way that frightened poor old Bill.

"Next night we found that he had learned to curse, for he came on a lot of us asleep in our bunks, and among them poor old Bill, and he pointed at us with a finger, and made a curse that our souls should stay all night at the top of the masts. And suddenly there was the soul of poor old Bill sitting like a monkey at the top of the mast, and looking at the stars, and freezing through and through.

"We got up a little mutiny after that, but Captain comes up and points with his finger again, and this time poor old Bill and all the rest are swimming behind the ship through the cold, green water, though their bodies remain on deck.

"It was the cabin-boy who found out that Captain couldn't curse when he was drunk, though he could shoot as well at one time as another.

"After that it was only a matter of waiting, and of losing two men when the time came. Some of us were murderous fellows, and wanted to kill Captain, but poor old Bill was for finding a bit of an island, out of the track of ships, and leaving him there with his share of our year's provisions. And everybody listened to poor old Bill, and we decided to maroon Captain as soon as we caught him when he couldn't curse.

"It was three whole days before Captain got drunk again, and poor old Bill and all had a dreadful time, for Captain invented new curses every day, and wherever he pointed his finger our souls had to go; and the fishes got to know us, and so did the stars, and none of them pitied us when we froze on the masts or were hurried through forests of seaweed and lost our way—both stars and fishes went about their businesses with cold, unastonished eyes. Once when the sun had set and it was twilight, and the moon was showing clearer and clearer in the sky, and we stopped our work for a moment because Captain seemed to be looking away from us at the colours in the sky, he suddenly turned and sent our souls to the Moon. And it was colder there than ice at night; and there were horrible mountains making shadows; and it was all as silent as miles of tombs; and Earth was shining up in the sky as big as the blade of a scythe, and we all got homesick for it, but could not speak nor cry. It was quite dark when we got back, and we were very respectful to Captain all the next day, but he cursed several of us again very soon. What we all feared most was that he would curse our souls to Hell, and none of us mentioned Hell above a whisper for fear that it should remind him. But on the third evening the cabin-boy came and told us that Captain was drunk. And we all went to his cabin, and we found him lying there across his bunk, and he shot as he had never shot before; but he had no more than the two pistols, and he would only have killed two men if he hadn't caught Joe over the head with the end of one of his pistols. And then we tied him up. And poor old Bill put the rum between Captain's teeth, and kept him drunk for two days, so that he could not curse, till we found a convenient rock. And before sunset of the second day we found a nice bare island for Captain, out of the track of ships, about a hundred yards long and about eighty wide; and we rowed him along to it in a little boat, and gave him provisions for a year, the same as we had ourselves, because poor old Bill wanted to be fair. And we left him sitting comfortable with his back to a rock singing a sailor's song.

"When we could no longer hear Captain singing we all grew very cheerful and made a banquet out of our year's provisions, as we all hoped to be home again in under three weeks. We had three great banquets every day for a week —every man had more than he could eat, and what was left over we threw on the floor like gentlemen. And then one day, as we saw San Huëlgédos, and wanted to sail in to spend our money, the wind changed round from behind us and beat us out to sea. There was no tacking against it, and no getting into the harbor, though other ships sailed by us and anchored there. Sometimes a dead calm would fall on us, while fishing boats all around us flew before half a gale, and sometimes the wind would beat us out to sea when nothing else was moving. All day we tried, and at night we laid to and tried again next day. And all the sailors of the other ships were spending their money in San Huëlgédos and we could not come nigh it. Then we spoke horrible things against the wind and against San Huëlgédos, and sailed away.

"It was just the same at Norenna.

"We kept close together now and talked in low voices. Suddenly poor old Bill grew frightened. As we went all along the Siractic coast-line, we tried again and again, and the wind was waiting for us in every harbour and sent us out to sea. Even the little islands would not have us. And then we knew that there was no landing yet for poor old Bill, and every one upbraided his kind heart that had made them maroon Captain on a rock, so as not to have his blood upon their heads. There was nothing to do but to drift about the seas. There were no banquets now, because we feared that Captain might live his year and keep us out to sea.

"At first we used to hail all passing ships, and used to try to board them in the boats; but there was no rowing against

Captain's curse, and we had to give that up. So we played cards for a year in Captain's cabin, night and day, storm and fine, and every one promised to pay poor old Bill when we got ashore.

"It was horrible to us to think what a frugal man Captain really was, he that used to get drunk every other day whenever he was at sea, and here he was still alive, and sober, too, for his curse still kept us out of every port, and our provisions were gone.

"Well, it came to drawing lots, and Jim was the unlucky one. Jim only kept us about three days, and then we drew lots again, and this time it was the nigger. The nigger didn't keep us any longer, and we drew again, and this time it was Charlie, and still Captain was alive.

"As we got fewer one of us kept us longer. Longer and longer a mate used to last us, and we all wondered how ever Captain did it. It was five weeks over the year when, we drew Mike, and he kept us for a week, and Captain was still alive. We wondered he didn't get tired of the same old curse; but we supposed things looked different when one is alone on an island.

"When there was only Jakes and poor old Bill and the cabin-boy and Dick, we didn't draw any longer. We said that the cabin-boy had had all the luck, and he mustn't expect any more. Then poor old Bill was alone with Jakes and Dick, and Captain was still alive. When there was no more boy, and the Captain still alive, Dick, who was a huge, strong man like poor old Bill, said that it was Jakes' turn, and he was very lucky to have lived as long as he had. But poor old Bill talked it all over with Jakes, and they thought it better that Dick should take his turn.

"Then there was Jakes and poor old Bill; and Captain would not die.

"And these two used to watch one another night and day, when Dick was gone and no one else was left to them. And at last poor old Bill fell down in a faint and lay there for an hour. Then Jakes came up to him slowly with his knife, and makes a stab at poor old Bill as he lies there on the deck. And poor old Bill caught hold of him by the wrist, and put his knife into him twice to make quite sure, although it spoiled the best part of the meat. Then poor old Bill was all alone at sea.

"And the very next week, before the food gave out, Captain must have died on his bit of an island; for poor old Bill heard Captain's soul going cursing over the sea, and the day after that the ship was cast on a rocky coast.

"And Captain's been dead now for over a hundred years, and poor old Bill is safe ashore again. But it looks as if Captain hadn't done with him yet, for poor old Bill doesn't ever get any older, and somehow or other he doesn't seem to die. Poor old Bill!"

When this was over the man's fascination suddenly snapped, and we all jumped up and left him.

It was not only his revolting story, but it was the fearful look in the eyes of the man who told it, and the terrible ease with which his voice surpassed the roar of the rain, that decided me never again to enter that haunt of sailors— the tavern of the sea.

THE BEGGARS

I WAS walking down Piccadilly not long ago, thinking of
   nursery rhymes and regretting old romance.

As I saw the shopkeepers walk by in their black frock-
coats and their black hats, I thought of the old line in nursery annals, "The merchants of London, they wear scarlet."

The streets were all so unromantic, dreary. Nothing could
be done for them, I thought—nothing. And then my
thoughts were interrupted by barking dogs. Every dog in
the street seemed to be barking—every kind of dog, not
only the little ones but the big ones too. They were all
facing East towards the way I was coming by. Then I
turned round to look and had this vision, in Piccadilly, on
the opposite side to the houses just after you pass the cab-
rank.

Tall, bent men were coming down the street arrayed in
marvellous cloaks. All were sallow of skin and swarthy of
hair, and the most of them wore strange beards. They were
coming slowly, and they walked with staves, and their hands
were out for alms.

All the beggars had come to town.

I would have given them a gold doubloon engraven with
the towers of Castille, but I had no such coin. They did
not seem the people to whom it were fitting to offer the same
coin as one tendered for the use of a taxicab (O marvellous
ill-made word, surely the pass-word somewhere of some evil
order). Some of them wore purple cloaks with wide green

78

borders, and the border of green was a narrow strip with some, and some wore cloaks of old and faded red, and some wore violet cloaks, and none wore black. And they begged gracefully, as gods might beg for souls.

I stood by a lamp-post, and they came up to it, and one addressed it, calling the lamp-post brother, and said, "O lamp-post, our brother of the dark, are there many wrecks by thee in the tides of night? Sleep not, brother, sleep not. There were many wrecks and it were not for thee."

It was strange: I had not thought of the majesty of the street lamp and his long watching over drifting men. But he was not beneath the notice of these cloaked strangers.

And then one murmured to the street: "Art thou weary, street? Yet a little longer they shall go up and down, and keep thee clad with tar and wooden bricks. Be patient, street. In a while the earthquake cometh."

"Who are you?" people said. "And where do you come from?"

"Who may tell what we are," they answered, "or whence we come?"

And one turned towards the smoke-stained houses, saying, "Blessed be the houses, because men dream therein."

Then I perceived, what I had never thought, that all these staring houses were not alike, but different one from another, because they held different dreams.

And another turned to a tree that stood by the Green Park railings, saying, "Take comfort, tree, for the fields shall come again."

And all the while the ugly smoke went upwards, the smoke that has stifled Romance and blackened the birds. This, I thought, they can neither praise nor bless. And when they saw it they raised their hands towards it, towards the thousand chimneys, saying, "Behold the smoke. The old coal-forests that have lain so long in the dark, and so long still, are dancing now and going back to the sun. Forget not Earth, O our brother, and we wish thee joy of the sun."

It had rained, and a cheerless stream dropped down a dirty gutter. It had come from heaps of refuse, foul and forgotten; it had gathered upon its way things that were derelict, and went to sombre drains unknown to man or the sun. It was this sullen stream as much as all other causes that had made me say in my heart that the town was vile, that Beauty was dead in it, and Romance fled.

Even this thing they blessed. And one that wore a purple cloak with broad green border, said, "Brother, be hopeful yet, for thou shalt surely come at last to the delectable Sea, and meet the heaving, huge, and travelled ships, and rejoice by isles that know the golden sun." Even thus they blessed the gutter, and I felt no whim to mock.

And the people that went by, in their black, unseemly coats and their misshapen, monstrous, shiny hats, the beggars also blessed. And one of them said to one of these dark citizens: "O twin of Night himself, with thy specks of white at wrists and neck like to Night's scattered stars. How fearfully thou dost veil with black thy hid, unguessed desires. They are deep thoughts in thee that they will not frolic with colour, that they say 'No' to purple, and to lovely green 'Begone.' Thou hast wild fancies that they must needs be tamed with black, and terrible imaginings that they must be hidden thus. Has thy soul dreams of the angels, and of the walls of faëry that thou has guarded it so utterly, lest it dazzle astonished eyes? Even so God hid the diamond deep down in miles of clay.

The wonder of thee is not marred by mirth.

Behold thou art very secret.

Be wonderful. Be full of mystery."

Silently the man in the black frock-coat passed on. And I came to understand when the purple beggar had spoken, that the dark citizen had trafficked perhaps with Ind, that in his heart were strange and dumb ambitions: that his dumbness was founded by solemn rite on the roots of ancient tradition: that it might be overcome one day by a cheer in the street or by some one singing a song, and that when this shopman spoke there might come clefts in the world and people peering over at the abyss.

Then turning towards Green Park, where as yet Spring was not, the beggars stretched out their hands, and looking at the frozen grass and the yet unbudding trees they, chanting all together, prophesied daffodils.

A motor omnibus came down the street, nearly running over some of the dogs that were barking ferociously still. It was sounding its horn noisily.

And the vision went then.

CARCASSONNE

*In a letter from a friend whom I have never seen, one o[f]
those that read my books, this line was quoted—"But he[?]
he never came to Carcassonne." I do not know the origin[n]
of the line, but I made this tale about it.*

WHEN Camorak reigned at Arn, and the world was[s]
fairer, he gave a festival to all the Weald to com-[?]
memorate the splendour of his youth.

They say that his house at Arn was huge and high, and[d]
its ceiling painted blue; and when evening fell men would[d]
climb up by ladders and light the scores of candles hanging[g]
from slender chains. And they say, too, that sometimes a[?]
cloud would come, and pour in through the top of one of[f]
the oriel windows, and it would come over the edge[e]
of the stonework as the sea-mist comes over a sheer cliff's[s]
shaven lip where an old wind has blown forever and ever[r]
(he has swept away thousands of leaves and thousands o[f]
centuries, they are all one to him, he owes no allegiance t[o]
Time). And the cloud would re-shape itself in the hall's[s]
lofty vault and drift on through it slowly, and out to the sky[y]
again through another window. And from its shape the[e]
knights in Camorak's hall would prophesy the battles and[d]
sieges of the next season of war. They say of the hall of[f]
Camorak at Arn that there hath been none like it in any[y]
land, and foretell that there will be never.

Hither had come in the folk of the Weald from sheep-fold and from forest, revolving slow thoughts of food, and shelter, and love, and they sat down wondering in that famous hall; and therein also were seated the men of Arn, the town that clustered round the King's high house, and was all roofed with the red, maternal earth.

If old songs may be trusted, it was a marvellous hall.

Many who sat there could only have seen it distantly before, a clear shape in the landscape, but smaller than a hill. Now they beheld along the wall the weapons of Camorak's men, of which already the lute-players made songs, and tales were told at evening in the byres. There they descried the shield of Camorak that had gone to and fro across so many battles, and the sharp but dinted edges of his sword; there were the weapons of Gadriol the Leal, and Norn, and Athoric of the Sleety Sword, Heriel the Wild, Yarold, and Thanga of Esk, their arms hung evenly all round the hall, low where a man could reach them; and in the place of honour in the midst, between the arms of Camorak and of Gadriol the Leal, hung the harp of Arleon. And of all the weapons hanging on those walls none were more calamitous to Camorak's foes than was the harp of Arleon. For to a man that goes up against a strong place on foot, pleasant indeed is the twang and jolt of some fearful engine of war that his fellow-warriors are working behind him, from which huge rocks go sighing over his head and plunge among his foes; and pleasant to a warrior in the wavering fight are the swift commands of his King, and a joy to him are his comrades' distant cheers exulting suddenly at a turn of the war. All this and more was the harp to Camorak's men; for not only would it cheer his warriors on, but many a time would Arleon of the Harp strike wild amazement into opposing hosts by some rapturous prophecy suddenly shouted out while his hand swept over the roaring strings. Moreover, no war was ever declared till Camorak and his men has listened long to the harp, and were elate with the music and mad against peace. Once Arleon, for the sake of a rhyme, had made war upon Estabonn; and an evil king was overthrown, and honour and glory won; from such queer motives does good sometimes accrue.

Above the shields and the harps all round the hall were the painted figures of heroes of fabulous famous songs. Too trivial, because too easily surpassed by Camorak's men, seemed all the victories that the earth had known; neither was any trophy displayed of Camorak's seventy battles, for these were as nothing to his warriors or him compared with those things that their youth had dreamed and which they mightily purposed yet to do.

Above the painted pictures there was darkness, for evening was closing in, and the candles swinging on their slender chain were not yet lit in the roof; it was as though a piece of the night had been builded in to the edifice like a huge natural rock that juts into a house. And there sat all the warriors of Arn and the Weald-folk wondering at them; and none were more than thirty, and all were skilled in war. And Camorack sat at the head of all, exulting in his youth.

We must wrestle with Time for some seven decades, and he is a weak and puny antagonist in the first three bouts.

Now there was present at this feast a diviner, one who knew the schemes of Fate, and he sat among the people of the Weald and had no place of honour, for Camorak and his men had no fear of Fate. And when the meat was eaten and the bones cast aside, the king rose up from his chair, and having drunken wine, and being in the glory of his youth and with all his knights about him, called to the diviner, saying, "Prophesy."

And the diviner rose up, stroking his grey beard, and spake guardedly—"There are certain events," he said, "upon the ways of Fate that are veiled even from a diviner's eyes, and many more as clear to us that were better veiled from all; much I know that is better unforetold, and some things that I may not foretell on pain of centuries of punishment.

But this I know and foretell—that you will never come to Carcassonne."

Instantly there was a buzz of talk telling of Carcassonne—some had heard of it in speech or song, some had read of it, and some had dreamed of it. And the king sent Arleon of the Harp down from his right hand to mingle with the Weald-folk to hear aught that any told of Carcassonne. But the warriors told of the places they had won to—many a hard-held fortress, many a far-off land, and swore that they would come to Carcassonne.

And in a while came Arleon back to the king's right hand, and raised his harp and chanted and told of Carcassonne. Far away it was, and far and far away, a city of gleaming ramparts rising one over the other, and marble terraces behind the ramparts, and fountains shimmering on the terraces. To Carcassonne the elf-kings with their fairies had first retreated from men, and had built it on an evening late in May by blowing their elfin horns. Carcassonne! Carcassonne!

Travellers had seen it sometimes like a clear dream, with the sun glittering on its citadel upon a far-off hill-top, and then the clouds had come or a sudden mist; no one had seen it long or come quite close to it; though once there were some men that came very near, and the smoke from the houses blew into their faces, a sudden gust—no more, and these declared that some one was burning cedarwood there. Men had dreamed that there is a witch there, walking alone through the cold courts and corridors of marmorean palaces, fearfully beautiful still for all her fourscore centuries, singing the second oldest song, which was taught her by the sea, shedding tears for loneliness from eyes that would madden armies, yet will she not call her dragons home—Carcassonne is terribly guarded. Sometimes she swims in a marble bath through whose deeps a river tumbles, or lies all morning on the edge of it to dry slowly in the sun, and watches the heaving river trouble the deeps of the bath. It flows through the caverns of earth for further than she knows, and coming to light in the witch's bath goes down through the earth again to its own peculiar sea.

In autumn sometimes it comes down black with snow that spring has molten in unimagined mountains, or with ered blooms of mountain shrubs go beautifully by.

When there is blood in the bath she knows there is war in the mountains; and yet she knows not where those mountains are.

When she sings the fountains dance up from the dark earth, when she combs her hair they say there are storms at sea, when she is angry the wolves grow brave and all come down to the byres, when she is sad the sea is sad, and both are sad forever. Carcassonne! Carcassonne!

This city is the fairest of the wonders of Morning; the sun shouts when he beholdeth it; for Carcassonne Evening weepeth when Evening passeth away.

And Arleon told how many goodly perils were round about the city, and how the way was unknown, and it was a knightly venture. Then all the warriors stood up and sang of the splendour of the venture. And Camorak swore by the gods that had builded Arn, and by the honour of his warriors that, alive or dead, he would come to Carcassonne.

But the diviner rose and passed out of the hall, brushing the crumbs from him with his hands and smoothing his robe as he went.

Then Camorak said, "There are many things to be planned, and counsels to be taken, and provender to be gathered. Upon what day shall we start?" And all the warriors answering shouted, "Now." And Camorak smiled thereat, for he had but tried them. Down then from the walls they took their weapons, Sikorix, Kelleron, Aslof, Wole of the Axe; Huhenoth, Peace-breaker; Wolwuf, Father of War; Tarion, Lurth of the War-cry and many another. Little then dreamed the spiders that sat in that ringing hall of the unmolested leisure they were soon to enjoy.

When they were armed they all formed up and marched out of the hall, and Arleon strode before them singing of Carcassonne.

But the folk of the Weald arose and went back well-fed to their byres. They had no need of wars or of rare perils. They were ever at war with hunger. A long drought or hard winter were to them pitched battles; if the wolves entered a sheep-fold it was like the loss of a fortress, a thunder-storm on the harvest was like an ambuscade. Well-fed, they went back slowly to their byres, being at truce with hunger: and the night filled with stars.

And black against the starry sky appeared the round helms of the warriors as they passed the tops of the ridges, but in the valleys they sparkled now and then as the starlight flashed on steel.

They followed behind Arleon going south, whence rumours had always come of Carcassonne: so they marched in the starlight, and he before them singing.

When they had marched so far that they heard no sound from Arn, and even inaudible were her swinging bells, when candles burning late far up in towers no longer sent them their disconsolate welcome; in the midst of the pleasant night that lulls the rural spaces, weariness came upon Arleon and his inspiration failed. It failed slowly. Gradually he grew less sure of the way to Carcassonne. Awhile he stopped to think, and remembered the way again; but his clear certainty was gone, and in its place were efforts in his mind to recall old prophecies and shepherd's songs that told of the marvellous city. Then as he said over carefully to himself a song that a wanderer had learnt from a goat-herd's boy far up the lower slope of ultimate southern mountains, fatigue came down upon his toiling mind like snow on the winding ways of a city noisy by night, stilling all.

He stood, and the warriors closed up to him. For long they had passed by great oaks standing solitary here and there, like giants taking huge breaths of the night air before doing some furious deed; now they had come to the verge of a black forest; the tree-trunks stood like those great columns in an Egyptian hall whence God in an older mood received the praise of men; the top of it sloped the way of an ancient wind. Here they all halted and lighted a fire of branches, striking sparks from flint into a heap of bracken. They eased them of their armour, and sat round the fire, and Camorak stood up there and addressed them, and Camorak said: "We go to war with Fate, who has doomed that I shall not come to Carcassonne. And if we turn aside but one of the dooms of Fate, then the whole future of the world is ours, and the future that Fate has ordered is like the dry course of an averted river. But if such men as we, such resolute conquerors, cannot prevent one doom that Fate has planned, then is the race of man enslaved forever to do its petty and allotted task."

Then they all drew their swords, and waved them high in the firelight, and declared war on Fate.

Nothing in the sombre forest stirred or made any sound.

Tired men do not dream of war. When morning came over the gleaming fields a company that had set out from Arn discovered the camping-place of the warriors, and brought pavilions and provender. And the warriors feasted, and the birds in the forest sang, and the inspiration of Arleon awoke.

Then they arose, and following Arleon, entered the forest, and marched away to the South. And many a woman of Arn sent her thoughts with them as they played alone some old monotonous tune, but their own thoughts were far before them, skimming over the bath through whose deeps the river tumbles in marble Carcassonne.

When butterflies were dancing on the air, and the sun neared the zenith, pavilions were pitched, and all the warriors rested; and then they feasted again, and then played knightly games, and late in the afternoon marched on once more, singing of Carcassonne.

And night came down with its mystery on the forest, and gave their demoniac look again to the trees, and rolled up out of misty hollows a huge and yellow moon.

And the men of Arn lit fires, and sudden shadows arose and leaped fantastically away. And the night-wind blew, arising like a ghost, and passed between the tree-trunks, and slipped down shimmering glades, and waked the prowling beasts still dreaming of day, and drifted nocturnal birds afield to menace timorous things, and beat the roses against cottagers' panes, and whispered news of the befriending night, and wafted to the ears of wandering men the sound of a maiden's song, and gave a glamour to the lutanist's tune played in his loneliness on distant hills; and the deep eyes of moths glowed like a galleon's lamps, and they spread their wings and sailed their familiar sea. Upon this night-wind also the dreams of Camorak's men floated to Carcassonne.

All the next morning they marched, and all the evening, and knew they were nearing now the deeps of the forest. And the citizens of Arn kept close together and close behind the warriors. For the deeps of the forest were all unknown to travellers, but not unknown to those tales of fear that men tell at evening to their friends, in the comfort and the safety of their hearths. Then night appeared, and an enormous moon. And the men of Camorak slept. Sometimes they woke, and went to sleep again; and those that stayed awake for long and listened heard heavy two-footed creatures pad through the night on paws.

As soon as it was light the unarmed men of Arn began to slip away, and went back by bands through the forest. When darkness came they did not stop to sleep, but continued their flight straight on until they came to Arn, and added there by the tales they told to the terror of the forest.

But the warriors feasted, and afterwards Arleon rose, and played his harp, and led them on again; and a few faithful servants stayed with them still. And they marched all day through a gloom that was as old as night, but Arleon's inspiration burned in his mind like a star. And he led them till the birds began to drop into the tree-tops, and it was evening and they all encamped. They had only one pavilion left to them now, and near it they lit a fire, and Camorak posted a sentry with drawn sword just beyond the glow of the firelight. Some of the warriors slept in the pavilion and others round about it.

When dawn came something terrible had killed and eaten the sentry. But the splendour of the rumours of Carcassonne and Fate's decree that they should never come there, and the inspiration of Arleon and his harp, all urged the warriors on; and they marched deeper and deeper all day into the forest.

Once they saw a dragon that had caught a bear and was playing with it, letting it run a little way and overtaking it with a paw.

They came at last to a clear space in the forest just before nightfall. An odour of flowers arose from it like a mist, and every drop of dew interpreted heaven unto itself.

It was the hour when twilight kisses Earth.

It was the hour when a meaning comes into senseless things, and trees out-majesty the pomp of monarchs, and the timid creatures steal abroad to feed, and as yet the beasts of prey harmlessly dream, and Earth utters a sigh, and it is night.

In the midst of the wide clearing Camorak's warriors camped, and rejoiced to see the stars again appearing one by one.

That night they ate the last of their provisions, and slept unmolested by the prowling things that haunt the gloom of the forest.

On the next day some of the warriors hunted stags, and others lay in rushes by a neighbouring lake and shot arrows at water-fowl. One stag was killed, and some geese, and several teal.

Here the adventurers stayed, breathing the pure wild air that cities know not; by day they hunted, and lit fires by night, and sang and feasted, and forgot Carcassonne. The terrible denizens of the gloom never molested them, venison was plentiful, and all manner of water-fowl: they loved the chase by day, and by night their favourite songs. Thus day after day went by, thus week after week. Time flung over this encampment a handful of noons, the gold and silver moons that waste the year away; Autumn and Winter passed, and Spring appeared; and still the warriors hunted and feasted there.

One night of the springtide they were feasting about a fire and telling tales of the chase, and the soft moths came out of the dark and flaunted their colours in the firelight, and went out grey into the dark again; and the night wind was cool upon the warriors' necks, and the camp-fire was warm in their faces, and a silence had settled among them after some song, and Arleon all at once rose suddenly up, remembering Carcassonne. And his hand swept over the strings of his harp, awaking the deeper chords, like the sound of a nimble people dancing their steps on bronze, and the music rolled away into the night's own silence, and the voice of Arleon rose:

"When there is blood in the bath she knows there is war in the mountains, and longs for the battle-shout of kingly men."

And suddenly all shouted, "Carcassonne!" And at that word their idleness was gone as a dream is gone from a dreamer waked with a shout. And soon the great march began that faltered no more nor wavered. Unchecked by battles, undaunted in lonesome spaces, ever unwearied by the vulturous years, the warriors of Camorak held on; and Arleon's inspiration led them still. They cleft with the music of Arleon's harp the gloom of ancient silences; they went singing into battles with terrible wild men, and came out singing, but with fewer voices; they came to villages in valleys full of the music of bells, or saw the lights at dusk of cottages sheltering others.

They became a proverb for wandering, and a legend arose of strange, disconsolate men. Folks spoke of them at nightfall when the fire was warm and rain slipped down the eaves; and when the wind was high small children feared the Men Who Would Not Rest were going clattering past. Strange tales were told of men in old grey armour moving at twilight along the tops of the hills and never asking shelter; and mothers told their boys who grew impatient of home that the grey wanderers were once so impatient and were now hopeless of rest, and were driven along with the rain whenever the wind was angry.

But the wanderers were cheered in their wandering by the hope of coming to Carcassonne, and later on by anger against Fate, and at last they marched on still because it seemed better to march on than to think.

For many years they had wandered and had fought with many tribes; often they gathered legends in villages and listened to idle singers singing songs; and all the rumours of Carcassonne still came from the South.

And then one day they came to a hilly land with a legend in it that only three valleys away a man might see, on clear days, Carcassonne. Tired though they were and few, and worn with the years which had all brought them wars, they pushed on instantly, led still by Arlcon's inspiration which dwindled in his age, though he made music with his old harp still.

All day they climbed down into the first valley and for two days ascended, and came to the Town That May Not Be Taken In War below the top of the mountain, and its gates were shut against them, and there was no way round. To left and right steep precipices stood as far as eye could see or legend tell of, and the pass lay through the city. Therefore Camorak drew up his remaining warriors in line of battle to wage their last war, and they stepped forward over the crisp bones of old, unburied armies.

No sentinel defied them in the gate, no arrow flew from

any tower of war. One citizen climbed alone to the mountain's top, and the rest hid themselves in sheltered places.

Now, in the top of the mountain was a deep, bowl-like
cavern in the rock, in which fires bubbled softly. But if any
cast a boulder into the fires, as it was the custom for one
of those citizens to do when enemies approached them, the
mountain hurled up intermittent rocks for three days, and
the rocks fell flaming all over the town and all round about
it. And just as Camorak's men began to batter the gate they
heard a crash on the mountain, and a great rock fell beyond
them and rolled into the valley. The next two fell in front
of them on the iron roofs of the town. Just as they entered
the town a rock found them crowded in a narrow street,
and shattered two of them. The mountain smoked and
panted; with every pant a rock plunged into the streets or
bounced along the heavy iron roof, and the smoke went
slowly up, and up, and up.

When they had come through the long town's empty streets
to the locked gate at the end, only fifteen were left. When
they had broken down the gate there were only ten alive.
Three more were killed as they went up the slope, and two
as they passed near the terrible cavern. Fate let the rest
go some way down the mountain upon the other side, and
then took three of them. Camorak and Arleon alone were
left alive. And night came down on the valley to which they
had come, and was lit by flashes from the fatal mountain;
and the two mourned for their comrades all night long.

But when the morning came they remembered their war
with Fate, and their old resolve to come to Carcasonne, and
the voice of Arleon rose in a quavering song, and snatches of
music from his old harp, and he stood up and marched with
his face southwards as he had done for years, and behind
him Camorak went. And when at last they climbed from
the third valley, and stood on the hill's summit in the golden
sunlight of evening, their aged eyes saw only miles of forest
and the birds going to roost.

Their beards were white, and they had travelled very far and hard; it was the time with them when a man rests from labours and dreams in light sleep of the years that were and not of the years to come.

Long they looked southwards; and the sun set over remoter forests, and glow-worms lit their lamps, and the inspiration of Arleon rose and flew away forever, to gladden, perhaps, the dreams of younger men.

And Arleon said: "My King, I know no longer the way to Carcassonne."

And Camorak smiled, as the aged smile, with little cause for mirth, and said: "The years are going by us like huge birds, whom Doom and Destiny and the schemes of God have frightened up out of some old grey marsh. And it may well be that against these no warrior may avail, and that Fate has conquered us, and that our quest has failed."

And after this they were silent.

Then they drew their swords, and side by side went down into the forest, still seeking for Carcassonne.

I think they got not far; for there were deadly marshes in that forest, and gloom that outlasted the nights, and fearful beasts accustomed to its ways. Neither is there any legend, either in verse or among the songs of the people of the fields, of any having come to Carcassonne.

IN ZACCARATH

"COME," said the King in sacred Zaccarath, "and let our prophets prophesy before us."

A far-seen jewel of light was the holy palace, a wonder to the nomads on the plains.

There was the King with all his underlords, and the lesser kings that did him vassalage, and there were all his queens with all their jewels upon them.

Who shall tell of the splendour in which they sat; of the thousand lights and the answering emeralds; of the dangerous beauty of that hoard of queens, or the flash of their laden necks?

There was a necklace there of rose-pink pearls beyond the art of dreamer to imagine. Who shall tell of the amethyst chandeliers, where torches, soaked in rare Bhyrinian oils, burned and gave off a scent of blethany?*

Enough to say that when the dawn came up it appeared by contrast pallid and unlovely and stripped all bare of its glory, so that it hid itself with rolling clouds.

---

* The herb marvellous, which growing near the summit of Mount Zaumnos, scents all the Zaumnian range, and is smelt far out on the Kepuscran plains, and even, when the wind is from the mountains, in the streets of the city of Ognoth. At night it closes its petals and is heard to breathe, and its breath is a swift poison. This it does even by day if the snows are disturbed about it. No plant of this has ever been captured alive by a hunter.

"Come," said the King, "let our prophets prophesy."

Then the heralds stepped through the ranks of the King's silk-clad warriors who lay oiled and scented upon velvet cloaks, with a pleasant breeze among them caused by the fans of slaves; even their casting-spears were set with jewels; through their ranks the heralds went with mincing steps, and came to the prophets, clad in brown and black, and one of them they brought and set him before the King. And the King looked at him and said, "Prophesy unto us."

And the prophet lifted his head, so that his beard came clear from his brown cloak, and the fans of the slaves that fanned the warriors wafted the tip of it a little awry. And he spake to the King, and spake thus:

"Woe unto thee, King, and woe unto Zaccarath. Woe unto thee, and woe unto thy women, for your fall shall be sore and soon. Already in Heaven the gods shun thy god: they know his doom and what is written of him: he sees oblivion before him like a mist. Thou hast aroused the hate of the mountaineers. They hate thee all along the crags of Droom. The evilness of thy days shall bring down the Zeedians on thee as the suns of springtide bring the avalanche down. They shall do unto Zaccarath as the avalanche doth unto the hamlets of the valley." When the queens chattered or tittered among themselves, he merely raised his voice and still spake on: "Woe to these walls and the carven things upon them. The hunter shall know the camping-places of the nomads by the marks of the camp-fires on the plain, but he shall not know the place of Zaccarath."

A few of the recumbent warriors turned their heads to glance at the prophet when he ceased. Far overhead the echoes of his voice hummed on awhile among the cedarn rafters.

"Is he not splendid?" said the King. And many of that assembly beat with their palms upon the polished floor in token of applause. Then the prophet was conducted back to his place at the far end of that mighty hall, and for a while musicians played on marvellous curved horns, while drums throbbed behind them hidden in a recess. The musicians were sitting cross-legged on the floor, all blowing their huge horns in the brilliant torchlight, but as the drums throbbed louder in the dark they arose and moved slowly nearer to the King. Louder and louder drummed the drums in the dark, and nearer and nearer moved the men with the horns, so that their music should not be drowned by the drums before it reached the King.

A marvellous scene it was when the tempestuous horns were halted before the King, and the drums in the dark were like the thunder of God; and the queens were nodding their heads in time to the music, with their diadems flashing like heavens of falling stars; and the warriors lifted their heads and shook, as they lifted them, the plumes of those golden birds which hunters wait for by the Liddian lakes, in a whole lifetime killing scarcely six, to make the crests that the warriors wore when they feasted in Zaccarath. Then the King shouted and the warriors sang—almost they remembered then old battle-chants. And, as they sang, the sound of the drums dwindled, and the musicians walked away backwards, and the drumming became fainter and fainter as they walked, and altogether ceased, and they blew no more on their fantastic horns. Then the assemblage beat on the floor with their palms. And afterwards the queens besought the King to send for another prophet. And the heralds brought a singer, and placed him before the King; and the singer was a young man with a harp. And he swept the strings of it, and when there was silence he sang of the iniquity of the King. And he foretold the onrush of the Zeedians, and the fall and the forgetting of Zaccarath, and the coming again of the desert to its own, and the playing about of little lion cubs where the courts of the palace had stood.

"Of what is he singing?" said a queen to a queen.

"He is singing of everlasting Zaccarath."

As the singer ceased the assemblage beat listlessly on the floor, and the King nodded to him, and he departed.

When all the prophets had prophesied to them and all the singers sung, that royal company arose and went to other chambers, leaving the hall of festival to the pale and lonely dawn. And alone were left the lion-headed gods that were carven out of the walls; silent they stood, and their rocky arms were folded. And shadows over their faces moved like curious thoughts as the torches flickered and the dull dawn crossed the fields. And the colours began to change in the chandeliers.

When the last lutanist fell asleep the birds began to sing.

Never was greater splendour or a more famous hall. Wnen the queens went away through the curtained door with all their diadems, it was as though the stars should arise in their stations and troop together to the West at sunrise.

And only the other day I found a stone that had undoubtedly been a part of Zaccarath, it was three inches long and an inch broad; I saw the edge of it uncovered by the sand. I believe that only three other pieces have been found like it.

THE FIELD

WHEN one has seen Spring's blossom fall in London, and Summer appear and ripen and decay, as it does early in cities, and one is in London still, then, at some moment or another, the country places lift their flowery heads and call to one with an urgent, masterful clearness, upland behind upland in the twilight like to some heavenly choir arising rank on rank to call a drunkard from his gambling-hell. No volume of traffic can drown the sound of it, no lure of London can weaken its appeal. Having heard it one's fancy is gone, and evermore departed, to some coloured pebble a-gleam in a rural brook, and all that London can offer is swept from one's mind like some suddenly smitten metropolitan Goliath.

The call is from afar both in leagues and years, for the hills that call one are the hills that were, and their voices are the voices of long ago, when the elf-kings still had horns.

I see them now, those hills of my infancy (for it is they that call), with their faces upturned to the purple twilight, and the faint diaphanous figures of the fairies peering out from under the bracken to see if evening is come. I do not see upon their regal summits those desirable mansions, and highly desirable residences, which have lately been built for gentlemen who would exchange customers for tenants.

When the hills called I used to go to them by road, riding a bicycle. If you go by train you miss the gradual approach, you do not cast off London like an old forgiven sin, nor pass by little villages on the way that must have some rumour of the hills; nor, wondering if they are still the same, come at last upon the edge of their far-spread robes, and so on to their feet, and see far off their holy, welcoming faces. In the train you see them suddenly round a curve, and there they all are sitting in the sun.

I imagine that as one penetrated out from some enormous forest of the tropics, the wild beasts would become fewer, the gloom would lighten, and the horror of the place would slowly lift. Yet as one emerges nearer to the edge of London, and nearer to the beautiful influence of the hills, the houses become uglier, the streets viler, the gloom deepens, the errors of civilisation stand bare to the scorn of the fields.

Where ugliness reaches the height of its luxuriance, in the dense misery of the place, where one imagines the builder saying, "Here I culminate. Let us give thanks to Satan," there is a bridge of yellow brick, and through it, as through some gate of filigree silver opening on fairyland, one passes into the country.

To left and right, as far as one can see, stretches that monstrous city; before one are the fields like an oid, old song.

There is a field there that is full of king-cups. A stream runs through it, and along the stream is a little wood of oziers. There I used often to rest at the stream's edge before my long journey to the hills.

There I used to forget London, street by street. Sometimes I picked a bunch of king-cups to show them to the hills.

I often came there. At first I noticed nothing about the field except its beauty and its peacefulness.

But the second time that I came I thought there was something ominous about the field.

Down there among the king-cups by the little shallow stream I felt that something terrible might happen in just such a place.

I did not stay long there, because I thought that too much time spent in London had brought on these morbid fancies and I went on to the hills as fast as I could.

I stayed for some days in the country air, and when I came back I went to the field again to enjoy that peaceful spot before entering London. But there was still something ominous among the oziers.

A year elapsed before I went there again. I emerged from the shadow of London into the gleaming sun, the bright green grass and the king-cups were flaming in the light, and the little stream was singing a happy song. But the moment I stepped into the field my old uneasiness returned, and worse than before. It was as though the shadow was brooding there of some dreadful future thing, and a year had brought it nearer.

I reasoned that the exertion of bicycling might be bad for one, and that the moment one rested this uneasiness might result.

A little later I came back past the field by night, and the song of the stream in the hush attracted me down to it. And there the fancy came to me that it would be a terribly cold place to be in the starlight, if for some reason one was hurt and could not get away.

I knew a man who was minutely acquainted with the past history of that locality, and him I asked if anything historical had ever happened in that field. When he pressed me for my reason in asking him this, I said that the field had seemed to me such a good place to hold a pageant in. But he said that nothing of any interest had ever occurred there, nothing at all.

So it was from the future that the field's trouble came.

For three years off and on I made visits to the field, and every time more clearly it boded evil things, and my uneasiness grew more acute every time that I was lured to go and rest among the cool green grass under the beautiful oziers. Once to distract my thoughts I tried to gauge how fast the stream was trickling, but I found myself wondering if it flowed faster than blood.

I felt that it would be a terrible place to go mad in, one would hear voices.

At last I went to a poet whom I knew, and woke him from huge dreams, and put before him the whole case of the field. He had not been out of London all that year, and he promised to come with me and look at the field, and tell me what was going to happen there. It was late in July when we went. The pavement, the air, the houses and the dirt had been all baked dry by the summer, the weary traffic dragged on, and on, and on, and Sleep spreading her wings soared up and floated from London and went to walk beautifully in rural places.

When the poet saw the field he was delighted, the flowers were out in masses all along the stream, he went down to the little wood rejoicing. By the side of the stream he stood and seemed very sad. Once or twice he looked up and down it mournfully, then he bent and looked at the king-cups, first one and then another, very closely, and shaking his head.

For a long while he stood in silence, and all my old uneasiness returned, and my bodings for the future.

And then I said, "What manner of field is it?"

And he shook his head sorrowfully.

"It is a battlefield," he said.

THE DAY OF THE POLL

I n the town by the sea it was the day of the poll, and the
poet regarded it sadly when he woke and saw the light of
it coming in at his window between two small curtains of
gauze. And the day of the poll was beautifully bright;
stray bird-songs came to the poet at the window; the air
was crisp and wintry, but it was the blaze of sunlight that
had deceived the birds. He heard the sound of the sea that
the moon led up the shore, dragging the months away over
the pebbles and shingles and piling them up with the years
where the worn-out centuries lay; he saw the majestic downs
stand facing mightily southwards; he saw the smoke of the
town float up to their heavenly faces—column after column
rose calmly into the morning as house by house was waked
by peering shafts of the sunlight and lit its fires for the
day; column by column went up toward the serene downs'
faces, and failed before they came there and hung all white
over houses; and every one in the town was raving mad.

It was a strange thing that the poet did for he hired the
largest motor in the town and covered it with all the flags he
could find, and set out to save an intelligence. And he
presently found a man whose face was hot, who shouted that
the time was not far distant when a candidate, whom he
named, would be returned at the head of the poll by a
thumping majority. And by him the poet stopped and
offered him a seat in the motor that was covered with flags.
When the man saw the flags that were on the motor, and

103

that it was the largest in the town, he got in. He said that his vote should be given for that fiscal system that had made us what we are, in order that the poor man's food should not be taxed to make the rich man richer. Or else it was that he would give his vote for that system of tariff reform which should unite us closer to our colonies with ties that should long endure, and give employment to all. But it was not to the polling-booth that that motor went, it passed it and left the town and came by a small white winding road to the very top of the downs. There the poet dismissed the car and led that wondering voter on to the grass and seated himself on a rug. And for long the voter talked of those imperial traditions that our forefathers had made for us and which he should uphold with his vote, or else it was of a people oppressed by a feudal system that was out of date and effete, and that should be ended or mended. But the poet pointed out to him small, distant, wandering ships on the sunlit strip of sea, and the birds far down below them, and the houses below the birds, with the little columns of smoke that could not find the downs.

And at first the voter cried for his polling-booth like a child; but after a while he grew calmer, save when faint burst of cheering came twittering up to the downs, when the voter would cry out bitterly against the misgovernment of the Radical party, or else it was—I forget what the poet told me—he extolled its splendid record.

"See," said the poet, "these ancient beautiful things the downs and the oldtime houses and the morning, and the grey sea in the sunlight going mumbling round the world. And this is the place they have chosen to go mad in!"

And standing there with all broad England behind him, rolling northward, down after down, and before him the glittering sea too far for the sound of the roar of it, there seemed to the voter to grow less important the questions that troubled the town. Yet he was still angry.

"Why did you bring me here?" he said again.

"Because I grew lonely," said the poet, "when all the town went mad."

Then he pointed out to the voter some old bent thorns, and showed him the way that a wind had blown for a million years, coming up at dawn from the sea; and he told him of the storms that visit the ships, and their names and whence they come, and the currents they drive afield, and the way that the swallows go. And he spoke of the down where they sat, when the summer came, and the flowers that were not yet, and the different butterflies, and about the bats and the swifts, and the thoughts in the heart of man. He spoke of the aged windmill that stood on the down, and of how to children it seemed a strange old man who was only dead by day. And as he spoke, and as the sea-wind blew on that high and lonely place, there began to slip away from the voter's mind meaningless phrases that had crowded it long—thumping majority—victory in the fight—terminological inexactitudes—and the smell of paraffin lamps dangling in heated schoolrooms, and quotations taken from ancient speeches because the words were long. They fell away, though slowly, and slowly the voter saw a wider world and the wonder of the sea. And the afternoon wore on, and the winter evening came, and the night fell, and all black grew the sea; and about the time that the stars come blinking out to look upon our littleness, the polling-booth closed in the town.

When they got back the turmoil was on the wane in the streets; night hid the glare of the posters; and the tide, finding the noise abated and being at the flow, told an old tale that he had learned in his youth about the deeps of the sea, the same which he had told to coastwise ships that brought it to Babylon by the way of Euphrates before the doom of Troy.

I blame my friend the poet, however lonely he was, for preventing this man from registering his vote (the duty of every citizen); but perhaps it matters less, as it was a foregone conclusion, because the losing candidate, either through poverty or sheer madness, had neglected to subscribe to a single football club.

THE UNHAPPY BODY

WHY do you not dance with us and rejoice with us?" they said to a certain body. And then that body made the confession of its trouble. It said: "I am united with a fierce and violent soul, that is altogether tyrannous and will not let me rest, and he drags me away from the dances of my kin to make me toil at his detestable work; and he will not let me do the little things, that would give pleasure to the folk I love, but only cares to please posterity when he has done with me and left me to the worms; and all the while he makes absurd demands of affection from those that are near to me, and is too proud even to notice any less than he demands, so that those that should be kind to me all hate me." And the unhappy body burst into tears.

And they said: "No sensible body cares for its soul. A soul is a little thing, and should not rule a body. You should drink and smoke more till he ceases to trouble you." But the body only wept, and said, "Mine is a fearful soul. I have driven him away for a little while with drink. But he will soon come back. Oh, he will soon come back!"

And the body went to bed hoping to rest, for it was drowsy with drink. But just as sleep was near it, it looked up, and there was its soul sitting on the windowsill, a misty blaze of light, and looking into the street.

"Come," said that tyrannous soul, "and look into the street."

"I have need of sleep," said the body.

"But the street is a beautiful thing," the soul said vehemently; "a hundred of the people are dreaming there."

"I am ill through want of rest," the body said.

"That does not matter," the soul said to it. "There are millions like you in the earth, and millions more to go there. The people's dreams are wandering afield; they pass the seas and the mountains of faëry, threading the intricate passes led by their souls; they come to golden temples a-ring with a thousand bells; they pass up steep streets lit by paper lanterns, where the doors are green and small; they know their way to witches' chambers and castles of enchantment; they know the spell that brings them to the causeway along the ivory mountains—on one side looking downward they behold the fields of their youth and on the other lie the radiant plains of the future. Arise and write down what the people dream."

"What reward is there for me," said the body, "if I write down what you bid me?"

"There is no reward," said the soul.

"Then I shall sleep," said the body.

And the soul began to hum an idle song sung by a young man in a fabulous land as he passed a golden city (where fiery sentinels stood), and knew that his wife was within it, though as yet but a little child, and knew by prophecy that furious wars, not yet arisen in far and unknown mountains should roll above him with their dust and thirst before he ever came to that city again—the young man sang it as he passed the gate, and was now dead with his wife a thousand years.

"I cannot sleep for that abominable song," the body cried to the soul.

"Then do as you are commanded," the soul replied. And wearily the body took a pen again. Then the soul spoke merrily as he looked through the window. "There is a mountain lifting sheer above London, part crystal and part mist. Thither the dreamers go when the sound of the traffic has fallen. At first they scarcely dream because of the roar of it, but before midnight it stops, and turns, and ebbs with all its wrecks. Then the dreamers arise and scale the shimmering mountain, and at its summit find the galleons of dream. Thence some sail East, some West, some into the Past and some into the Future, for the galleons sail over the years as well as over the spaces, but mostly they head for the Past and the olden harbours, for thither the sighs of men are mostly turned, and the dreamships go before them, as the merchantmen before the continual trade-winds go down the African coast. I see the galleons even now raise anchor after anchor; the stars flash by them; they slip out of the night; their prows go gleaming into the twilight of memory, and night soon lies far off, a black cloud hanging low, and faintly spangled with stars, like the harbour and shore of some low-lying land seen afar with its harbour lights."

Dream after dream that soul related as he sat there by the window. He told of tropical forests seen by unhappy men who could not escape from London, and never would—forests made suddenly wondrous by the song of some passing bird flying to unknown eeries and singing an unknown song. He saw the old men lightly dancing to the tune of elfin pipes—beautiful dances with fantastic maidens—all night on moonlit imaginary mountains; he heard far off the music of glittering Springs; he saw the fairness of blossoms of apple and may thirty years fallen; he heard old voices —old tears came glistening back; Romance sat cloaked and crowned upon southern hills, and the soul knew him.

One by one he told the dreams of all that slept in that street. Sometimes he stopped to revile the body because it worked badly and slowly. Its chill fingers wrote as fast as they could, but the soul cared not for that. And so the night wore on till the soul heard tinkling in Oriental skies far footfalls of the morning.

"See now," said the soul, "the dawn that the dreamers dread. The sails of light are paling on those unwreckable galleons; the mariners that steer them slip back into fable and myth; that other sea the traffic is turning now at its ebb, and is about to hide its pallid wrecks, and to come swinging back, with its tumult, at the flow. Already the sunlight flashes in the gulfs behind the east of the world; the gods have seen it from their palace of twilight that they built above the sunrise; they warm their hands at its glow as it streams through their gleaming arches, before it reaches the world; all the gods are there that have ever been, and all the gods that shall be; they sit there in the morning, chanting and praising Man."

"I am numb and very cold for want of sleep," said the body.

"You shall have centuries of sleep," said the soul, "but you must not sleep now, for I have seen deep meadows with purple flowers flaming tall and strange above the brilliant grass, and herds of pure white unicorns that gambol there for joy, and a river running by with a glittering galleon on it, all of gold, that goes from an unknown inland to an unknown isle of the sea to take a song from the King of Over-the-Hills to the Queen of Far-Away.

"I will sing that song to you, and you shall write it down."

"I have toiled for you for years," the body said. "Give me now but one night's rest, for I am exceeding weary."

"Oh, go and rest. I am tired of you. I am off," said the soul.

And he arose and went, we know not whither. But the body they laid in the earth. And the next night at midnight the wraiths of the dead came drifting from their tombs to felicitate that body.

"You are free here, you know," they said to their new companion.

"Now I can rest," said the body.

THE SWORD OF WELLERAN

WHERE the great plain of Tarphet runs up, as the sea in estuaries, among the Cyresian mountains, there stood long since the city of Merimna well-nigh among the shadows of the crags. I have never seen a city in the world so beautiful as Merimna seemed to me when first I dreamed of it. It was a marvel of spires and figures of bronze, and marble fountains, and trophies of fabulous wars, and broad streets given over wholly to the Beautiful. Right through the centre of the city there went an avenue fifty strides in width, and along each side of it stood likenesses in bronze of the Kings of all the countries that the people of Marimna had ever known. At the end of that avenue was a colossal chariot with three bronze horses driven by the winged figure of Fame, and behind her in the chariot the huge form of Welleran, Merimna's ancient hero, standing with extended sword. So urgent was the mien and attitude of Fame, and so swift the pose of the horses, that you had sworn that the chariot was instantly upon you, and that its dust already veiled the faces of the Kings. And in the city was a mighty hall wherein were stored the trophies of Merimna's heroes. Sculptured it was and domed, the glory of the art of masons a long while dead, and on the summit of the dome the image of Rollory sat gazing across the Cyresian mountains toward the wide lands beyond, the lands that knew his sword. And beside Rollory, like an old nurse, the figure of Victory sat, hammering into a golden wreath of laurels for his head the crowns of fallen Kings.

Such was Merimna, a city of sculptured Victories and warriors of bronze. Yet in the time of which I write the art of war had been forgotten in Merimna, and the people almost slept. To and fro and up and down they would walk through the marble streets, gazing at memorials of the things achieved by their country's swords in the hands of those that long ago had loved Merimna well. Almost they slept, and dreamed of Welleran, Soorenard, Mommolek, Rollory, Akanax, and young Iraine. Of the lands beyond the mountains that lay all round about them they knew nothing, save that they were the theatre of the terrible deeds of Welleran, that he had done with his sword. Long since these lands had fallen back in the possession of the nations that had been scourged by Merimna's armies. Nothing now remained to Merimna's men save their inviolate city and the glory of the remembrance of their ancient fame. At night they would place sentinels far out in the desert, but these always slept at their posts dreaming of Rollory, and three times every night a guard would march around the city clad in purple, bearing lights and singing songs of Welleran. Always the guard went unarmed, but as the sound of their song went echoing across the plain towards the looming mountains, the desert robbers would hear the name of Welleran and steal away to their haunts. Often dawn would come across the plain, shimmering marvellously upon Merimna's spires, abashing all the stars, and find the guard still singing songs of Welleran, and would change the colour of their purple robes and pale the lights they bore. But the guard would go back leaving the ramparts safe, and one by one the sentinels in the plain would awake from dreaming of Rollory and shuffle back into the city quite cold. Then something of the menace would pass away from the faces of the Cyresian mountains, that from the north and the west and the south lowered upon Merimna, and clear in the morning the statues and the pillars would arise in the old inviolate city. You would wonder that an unarmed guard and sentinels that slept could defend a city that was stored with all the glories of art, that was rich in gold and bronze, a haughty city that had erst oppressed its neighbours, whose people had forgotten the art of war. Now this is the reason that, though all her other lands had long been taken from her, Merimna's city was safe. A strange thing was believed or feared by the fierce tribes beyond the mountains, and it was credited among them that at certain stations round Merimna's ramparts there still rode Welleran, Soorenard, Mommolek, Rollory, Akanax, and young Iraine. Yet it was close on a hundred years since Iraine, the youngest of Merimna's heroes, fought his last battle with the tribes.

Sometimes indeed there arose among the tribes young men who doubted and said: "How may a man for ever escape death?"

But graver men answered them: "Hear us, ye whose wisdom has discerned so much, and discern for us how a man may escape death when two score horsemen assail him with their swords, all of them sworn to kill him, and all of them sworn upon their country's gods; as often Welleran hath. Or discern for us how two men alone may enter a walled city by night, and bring away from it that city's king, as did Soorenard and Mommolek. Surely men that have escaped so many swords and so many sleety arrows shall escape the years and Time."

And the young men were humbled and became silent. Still, the suspicion grew. And often when the sun set on the Cyresian mountains, men in Merimna discerned the forms of savage tribesmen black against the light, peering towards the city.

All knew in Merimna that the figures round the ramparts were only statues of stone, yet even there a hope

lingered among a few that some day their old heroes would
come again, for certainly none had ever seen them die. Now
it had been the wont of these six warriors of old, as each
received his last wound and knew it to be mortal, to ride
away to a certain deep ravine and cast his body in, as
somewhere I have read great elephants do, hiding their
bones away from lesser beasts. It was a ravine steep and
narrow even at the ends, a great cleft into which no man
could come by any path. There rode Welleran alone, panting hard; and there later rode Soorenard and Mommolek,
Mommolek with a mortal wound upon him not to return
but Soorenard was unwounded and rode back alone from
leaving his dear friend resting among the mighty bones
of Welleran. And there rode Soorenard, when his day was
come, with Rollory and Akanax, and Rollory rode in the
middle and Soorenard and Akanax on either side. And
the long ride was a hard and weary thing for Soorenard and
Akanax, for they both had mortal wounds; but the long ride
was easy for Rollory, for he was dead. So the bones of
these five heroes whitened in an enemy's land, and very
still they were, though they had troubled cities, and none
knew where they lay saving only Iraine, the young captain
who was but twenty-five when Mommolek, Rollory and
Akanax rode away. And among them were strewn their
saddles and their bridles, and all the accoutrements of their
horses, lest any man should ever find them afterwards and
say in some foreign city: "Lo! the bridles or the saddles of
Merimna's captains, taken in war," but their beloved trusty
horses they turned free.

Forty years afterwards, in the hour of a great victory,
his last wound came upon Iraine, and the wound was terrible and would not close. And Iraine was the last of the
captains, and rode away alone. It was a long way to the
dark ravine, and Iraine feared that he would never come
to the resting-place of the old heroes, and he urged his
horse on swiftly, and clung to the saddle with his hands

nd often as he rode he fell asleep, and dreamed of earlier
ays, and of the times when he first rode forth to the great
ars of Welleran, and of the time when Welleran first
pake to him, and of the faces of Welleran's comrades
hen they led charges in the battle. And ever as he awoke
great longing arose in his soul as it hovered on his body's
rink, a longing to lie among the bones of the old heroes.
t last when he saw the dark ravine making a scar across
he plain, the soul of Iraine slipped out through his great
ound and spread its wings, and pain departed from the
oor hacked body and, still urging his horse forward, Iraine
ied. But the old true horse cantered on till suddenly
e saw before him the dark ravine and put his forefeet
ut on the very edge of it and stopped. Then the body
f Iraine came toppling forward over the right shoulder of
he horse, and his bones mingle and rest as the years go
y with the bones of Merimna's heroes.

Now there was a little boy in Merimna named Rold. I
aw him first, I, the dreamer, that sit before my fire asleep,
saw him first as his mother led him through the great hall
here stand the trophies of Merimna's heroes. He was five
ears old, and they stood before the great glass casket
herein lay the sword of Welleran, and his mother said:
The sword of Welleran." And Rold said: "What should
 man do with the sword of Welleran?" And his mother
nswered: "Men look at the sword and remember Welleran."
nd they went on and stood before the great red cloak of
Welleran, and the child said: "Why did Welleran wear this
reat red cloak?" And his mother answered: "It was the
ay of Welleran."

When Rold was a little older he stole out of his mother's
ouse quite in the middle of the night when all the world
as still, and Merimna asleep dreaming of Welleran, Soore-
ard, Mommolek, Rollory, Akanax, and young Iraine. And
e went down to the ramparts to hear the purple guard go
y singing of Welleran. And the purple guard came by

with lights, all singing in the stillness, and dark shapes o
in the desert turned and fled. And Rold went back aga
to his mother's house with a great yearning towards t
name of Welleran, such as men feel for very holy things.

And in time Rold grew to know the pathway all rou
the ramparts, and the six equestrian statues that were the
guarding Merimna still. These statues were not like oth
statues, they were so cunningly wrought of many-colour
marbles that none might be quite sure until very close th
they were not living men. There was a horse of dappl
marble, the horse of Akanax. The horse of Rollory was
alabaster, pure white, his armour was wrought out of a sto
that shone, and his horse-man's cloak was made of a blu
stone, very precious. He looked northward.

But the marble horse of Welleran was pure black, ar
there sat Welleran upon him looking solemnly westward
His horse it was whose cold neck Rold most loved to strok
and it was Welleran whom the watchers at sunset on th
mountains the most clearly saw as they peered towards th
city. And Rold loved the red nostrils of the great blac
horse and his rider's jasper cloak.

Now beyond the Cyresians the suspicion grew tha
Merimna's heroes were dead, and a plan was devised that
man should go by night and come close to the figures upc
the ramparts and see whether they were Welleran, Soor
nard, Mommolek, Rollory, Akanax, and young Iraine. Ar
all were agreed upon the plan, and many names were me
tioned of those who should go, and the plan matured f
many years. It was during these years that watchers clu
tered often at sunset upon the mountains but came no neare
Finally, a better plan was made, and it was decided that tw
men who had been by chance condemned to death should b
given a pardon if they went down into the plain by nig
and discovered whether or not Merimna's heroes lived. A
first the two prisoners dared not go, but after a while on
of them, Seejar, said to his companion, Sajar-Ho: "Se

now, when the King's axeman smites a man upon the neck that man dies."

And the other said that this was so. Then said Seejar: "And even though Welleran smite a man with his sword no more befalleth him than death."

Then Sajar-Ho thought for a while. Presently he said: "Yet the eye of the King's axeman might err at the moment of his stroke or his arm fail him, and the eye of Welleran hath never erred nor his arm failed. It were better to bide here."

Then said Seejar: "Maybe that Welleran is dead and that some other holds his place upon the ramparts, or even a statue of stone."

But Sajar-Ho made answer: "How can Welleran be dead when he even escaped from two score horsemen with swords that were sworn to slay him, and all sworn upon our country's gods?"

And Seejar said: "This story his father told my grandfather concerning Welleran. On the day that the fight was lost on the plains of Kurlistan he saw a dying horse near to the river, and the horse looked piteously toward the water but could not reach it. And the father of my grandfather saw Welleran go down to the river's brink and bring water from it with his own hand and give it to the horse. Now we are in as sore a plight as was that horse, and as near to death; it may be that Welleran will pity us, while the King's axeman cannot because of the commands of the King."

Then said Sajar-Ho: "Thou wast ever a cunning arguer. Thou broughtest us into this trouble with thy cunning and thy devices, we will see if thou canst bring us out of it. We will go."

So news was brought to the King that the two prisoners would go down to Merimna.

That evening the watchers led them to the mountain's edge, and Seejar and Sajar-Ho went down towards the plain by the way of a deep ravine, and the watchers watched them go. Presently their figures were wholly hid in the dusk. Then night came up, huge and holy, out of waste marshes to the eastwards and low lands and the sea; and the angels that watched over all men through the day closed their great eyes and slept, and the angels that watched over all men through the night awoke and ruffled their deep blue feathers and stood up and watched. But the plain became a thing of mystery filled with fears. So the two spies went down the deep ravine, and coming to the plain sped stealthily across it. Soon they came to the line of sentinels asleep upon the sand, and one stirred in his sleep calling on Rollory, and a great dread seized upon the spies and they whispered "Rollory lives," but they remembered the King's axeman and went on. And next they came to the great bronze statue of Fear, carved by some sculptor of the old glorious years in the attitude of flight towards the mountains, calling to her children as she fled. And the children of Fear were carved in the likeness of the armies of all the trans-Cyresian tribes with their backs towards Merimna, flocking after Fear. And from where he sat on his horse behind the ramparts the sword of Welleran was stretched out over their heads as ever it was wont. And the two spies kneeled down in the sand and kissed the huge bronze foot of the statue of Fear, saying: "O Fear, Fear." And as they knelt they saw lights far off along the ramparts coming nearer and nearer, and heard men singing of Welleran. And the purple guard came nearer and went by with their lights, and passed on into the distance round the ramparts still singing of Welleran. And all the while the two spies clung to the foot of the statue, muttering: "O Fear, Fear." But when they could hear the name of Welleran no more they arose and came to the ramparts and climbed over them and came at once upon the figure of Welleran, and they bowed low to the ground, and Seejar said: "O Welleran, we came to see whether thou didst yet live." And for a long while they waited with their faces to the earth. At last Seegar looked up towards Welleran's terrible sword, and it was still stretched out pointing to the carved armies that followed after Fear. And Seejar bowed to the ground again and touched the horse's hoof, and it seemed cold to him. And he moved his hand higher and touched the leg of the horse, and it seemed quite cold. At last he touched Welleran's foot, and the armour on it seemed hard and stiff. Then as Welleran moved not and spake not, Seejar climbed up at last and touched his hand, the terrible hand of Welleran, and it was marble. Then Seejar laughed aloud, and he and Sajar-Ho sped down the empty pathway and found Rollory, and he was marble too. Then they climbed down over the ramparts and went back across the plain, walking contemptuously past the figure of Fear, and heard the guard returning round the ramparts for the third time, singing of Welleran; and Seejar said: "Ay, you may sing of Welleran, but Welleran is dead and a doom is on your city."

And they passed on and found the sentinel still restless in the night and calling on Rollory. And Sajar-Ho muttered: "Ay, you may call on Rollory, but Rollory is dead and naught can save your city."

And the two spies went back alive to their mountains again, and as they reached them the first ray of the sun came up red over the desert behind Merimna and lit Merimna's spires. It was the hour when the purple guard were wont to go back into the city with their tapers pale and their robes a brighter colour, when the cold sentinels came shuffling in from dreaming in the desert; it was the hour when the desert robbers hid themselves away, going back to their mountain caves; it was the hour when gauze-winged insects are born that only live for a day; it was the hour when men die that are condemned to death; and in this hour a great peril, new and terrible, arose for Merimna and Merimna knew it not.

Then Seejar turning said: "See how red the dawn is and

how red the spires of Merimna. They are angry with Merimna in Paradise and they bode its doom."

So the two spies went back and brought the news to their King, and for a few days the Kings of those countries were gathering their armies together; and one evening the armies of four Kings were massed together at the top of the deep ravine, all crouching below the summit waiting for the sun to set. All wore resolute and fearless faces, yet inwardly every man was praying to his gods, unto each one in turn.

Then the sun set, and it was the hour when the bats and the dark creatures are abroad and the lions come down from their lairs, and the desert robbers go into the plains again, and fevers rise up winged and hot out of chill marshes, and it was the hour when safety leaves the thrones of Kings, the hour when dynasties change. But in the desert the purple guard came swinging out of Merimna with their lights to sing of Welleran, and the sentinels lay down to sleep.

Now into Paradise no sorrow may ever come, but may only beat like rain against its crystal walls, yet the souls of Merimna's heroes were half aware of some sorrow far away as some sleeper feels that some one is chilled and cold yet knows not in his sleep that it is he. And they fretted a little in their starry home. Then unseen there drifted earthward across the setting sun the souls of Welleran, Soorenard, Mommolek, Rollory, Akanax, and young Iraine. Already when they reached Merimna's ramparts it was just dark, already the armies of the four Kings had begun to move, jingling, down the deep ravine. But when the six warriors saw their city again, so little changed after so many years, they looked towards her with a longing that was nearer to tears than any that their souls had known before, crying to her:

"O Merimna, our city: Merimna, our walled city.

"How beautiful thou art with all thy spires, Merimna. For thee we left the earth, its kingdoms and little flowers, for thee we have come away for awhile from Paradise.

"It is very difficult to draw away from the face of God —it is like a warm fire, it is like dear sleep, it is like a great anthem, yet there is a stillness all about it, a stillness full of lights.

"We have left Paradise for awhile for thee, Merimna.

"Many women have we loved, Merimna, but only one city.

"Behold now all the people dream, all our loved people. How beautiful are dreams! In dreams the dead may live, even the long dead and the very silent. Thy lights are all sunk low, they have all gone out, no sound is in thy streets. Hush! Thou art like a maiden that shutteth up her eyes and is asleep, that draweth her breath softly and is quite still, being at ease and untroubled.

"Behold now the battlements, the old battlements. Do men defend them still as we defended them? They are worn a little, the battlements," and drifting nearer they peered anxiously. "It is not by the hand of man that they are worn, our battlements. Only the years have done it and indomitable Time. Thy battlements are like the girdle of a maiden, a girdle that is round about her. See now the dew upon them, they are like a jewelled girdle.

"Thou art in great danger, Merimna, because thou art so beautiful. Must thou perish to-night because we no more defend thee, because we cry out and none hear us, as the bruised lilies cry out and none have known their voices?"

Thus spake those strong-voiced battle-ordering captains, calling to their dear city, and their voices came no louder than the whispers of little bats that drift across the twilight in the evening. Then the purple guard came near, going round the ramparts for the first time in the night, and the old warriors called to them, "Merimna is in danger! Already her enemies gather in the darkness." But their voices were never heard because they were only wandering ghosts.

And the guard went by and passed unheeding away, stil' singing of Welleran.

Then said Welleran to his comrades: "Our hands can hold swords no more, our voices cannot be heard, we are stalwart men no longer. We are but dreams, let us go among dreams. Go all of you, and thou too, young Iraine, and trouble the dreams of all the men that sleep, and urge them to take the old swords of their grandsires that hang upon the walls, and to gather at the mouth of the ravine; and I will find a leader and make him take my sword."

Then they passed up over the ramparts and into their dear city. And the wind blew about, this way and that, as he went, the soul of Welleran who had upon his day withstood the charges of tempestuous armies. And the souls of his comrades, and with them young Iraine, passed up into the city and troubled the dreams of every man who slept and to every man the souls said in their dreams: "It is hot and still in the city. Go out now into the desert, into the cool under the mountains, but take with thee the old sword that hangs upon the wall for fear of the desert robbers."

And the god of that city sent up a fever over it, and the fever brooded over it and the streets were hot; and all that slept awoke from dreaming that it would be cool and pleasant where the breezes came down the ravine out of the mountains; and they took the old swords that their grandsires had, according to their dreams, for fear of the desert robbers. And in and out of dreams passed the souls of Welleran's comrades, and with them young Iraine, in great haste as the night wore on; and one by one they troubled the dreams of all Merimna's men and caused them to arise and go out armed, all save the purple guard who, heedless of danger, sang of Welleran still, for waking men cannot hear the souls of the dead.

But Welleran drifted over the roofs of the city till he came to the form of Rold lying fast asleep. Now Rold was grown strong and was eighteen years of age, and he was fair of hair and tall like Welleran, and the soul of Welleran hovered over him and went into his dreams as a butterfly flits through trellis-work into a garden of flowers, and the soul of Welleran said to Rold in his dreams: "Thou wouldst go and see again the sword of Welleran, the great curved sword of Welleran. Thou wouldst go and look at it in the night with the moonlight shining upon it."

And the longing of Rold in his dreams to see the sword caused him to walk still sleeping from his mother's house to the hall wherein were the trophies of the heroes. And the soul of Welleran urging the dreams of Rold caused him to pause before the great red cloak, and there the soul said among the dreams: "Thou art cold in the night; fling now a cloak around thee."

And Rold drew round about him the huge red cloak of Welleran. Then Rold's dreams took him to the sword, and the soul said to the dreams: "Thou hast a longing to hold the sword of Welleran: take up the sword in thy hand."

But Rold said: "What should a man do with the sword of Welleran?"

And the soul of the old captain said to the dreamer: "It is a good sword to hold: take up the sword of Welleran."

And Rold, still sleeping and speaking aloud, said: "It is not lawful; none may touch the sword."

And Rold turned to go. Then a great and terrible cry arose in the soul of Welleran, all the more bitter for that he could not utter it, and it went round and round his soul finding no utterance, like a cry evoked long since by some murderous deed in some old haunted chamber that whispers through the ages heard by none.

And the soul of Welleran cried out to the dreams of Rold: "Thy knees are tied! Thou art fallen in a marsh! Thou canst not move."

And the dreams of Rold said to him: "Thy knees are tied, thou art fallen in a marsh," and Rold stood still before the sword. Then the soul of the warrior wailed among Rold's dreams, as Rold stood before the sword.

"Welleran is crying for his sword, his wonderful curved sword. Poor Welleran, that once fought for Merimna, is crying for his sword in the night. Thou wouldst not keep Welleran without his beautiful sword when he is dead and cannot come for it, poor Welleran who fought for Merimna."

And Rold broke the glass casket with his hand and took the sword, the great curved sword of Welleran; and the soul of the warrior said among Rold's dreams: "Welleran is waiting in the deep ravine that runs into the mountains, crying for his sword."

And Rold went down through the city and climbed over the ramparts, and walked with his eyes wide open but still sleeping over the desert to the mountains.

Already a great multitude of Merimna's citizens were gathered in the desert before the deep ravine with old swords in their hands, and Rold passed through them as he slept holding the sword of Welleran, and the people cried in amaze to one another as he passed: "Rold hath the sword of Welleran!"

And Rold came to the mouth of the ravine, and there the voices of the people woke him. And Rold knew nothing that he had done in his sleep, and looked in amazement at the sword in his hand and said: "What art thou, thou beautiful thing? Lights shimmer in thee, thou art restless. It is the sword of Welleran, the curved sword of Welleran!"

And Rold kissed the hilt of it, and it was salt upon his lips with the battle-sweat of Welleran. And Rold said: "What should a man do with the sword of Welleran?"

And all the people wondered at Rold as he sat there with the sword in his hand muttering, "What should a man do with the sword of Welleran?"

Presently there came to the ears of Rold the noise of a jingling up in the ravine, and all the people, the people that knew naught of war, heard the jingling coming nearer in the night; for the four armies were moving on Merimna and not yet expecting an enemy. And Rold gripped upon the hilt of the great curved sword, and the sword seemed to lift a little. And a new thought came into the hearts of Merimna's people as they gripped their grandsires' swords. Nearer and nearer came the heedless armies of the four Kings, and old ancestral memories began to arise in the minds of Merimna's people in the desert with their swords in their hands sitting behind Rold. And all the sentinels were awake holding their spears, for Rollory had put their dreams to flight, Rollory that once could put to flight armies and now was but a dream struggling with other dreams.

And now the armies had come very near. Suddenly Rold leaped up, crying: "Welleran! And the sword of Welleran!" And the savage, lusting sword that had thirsted for a hundred years went up with the hand of Rold and swept through a tribesman's ribs. And with the warm blood all about it there came a joy into the curved soul of that mighty sword, like to the joy of a swimmer coming up dripping out of warm seas after living for long in a dry land. When they saw the red cloak and that terrible sword a cry ran through the tribal armies, "Welleran lives!" And there arose the sounds of the exulting of victorious men, and the panting of those that fled, and the sword singing softly to itself as it whirled dripping through the air. And the last that I saw of the battle as it poured into the depth and darkness of the ravine was the sword of Welleran sweeping up and falling, gleaming blue in the moonlight whenever it rose and afterwards gleaming red, and so disappearing into the darkness.

But in the dawn Merimna's men came back, and the sun arising to give new life to the world, shone instead upon the hideous things that the sword of Welleran had done. And Rold said: "O sword, sword! How horrible thou art! Thou art a terrible thing to have come among men. How many eyes shall look upon gardens no more because of thee? How many fields must go empty that might have been fair with cottages, white cottages with children all about them? How many valleys must go desolate that might have nursed warm hamlets, because thou hast slain long since the men that might have built them? I hear the wind crying against thee, thou sword! It comes from the empty valleys. It comes over the bare fields. There are children's voices in it. They were never born. Death brings an end to crying for those that had life once, but these must cry for ever. O sword! sword! why did the gods send thee among men?" And the tears of Rold fell down upon the proud sword but could not wash it clean.

And now that the ardour of battle had passed away, the spirits of Merimna's people began to gloom a little, like their leader's, with their fatigue and with the cold of the morning; and they looked at the sword of Welleran in Rold's hand and said: "Not any more, not any more for ever will Welleran now return, for his sword is in the hand of another. Now we know indeed that he is dead. O Welleran, thou wast our sun and moon and all our stars. Now is the sun fallen down and the moon broken, and all the stars are scattered as the diamonds of a necklace that is snapped off one who is slain by violence."

Thus wept the people of Merimna in the hour of their great victory, for men have strange moods, while beside them their old inviolate city slumbered safe. But back from the ramparts and beyond the mountains and over the lands that they had conquered of old, beyond the world and back again to Paradise, went the souls of Welleran, Soorenard, Mommolek, Rollory, Akanax, and young Iraine.

THE FALL OF BABBULKUND

I SAID: "I will arise now and see Babbulkund, City of
Marvel. She is of one age with the earth; the stars
are her sisters. Pharaohs of the old time coming conquer-
ing from Araby first saw her, a solitary mountain in the
desert, and cut the mountain into towers and terraces.
They destroyed one of the hills of God, but they made Babbulkund. She is carven, not built; her palaces are one with
her terraces, there is neither join nor cleft. Hers is the
beauty of the youth of the world. She deemeth herself to
be the middle of Earth, and hath four gates facing outward
to the Nations. There sits outside her eastern gate a colossal god of stone. His face flushes with the lights of dawn.
When the morning sunlight warms his lips they part a
little, and he giveth utterance to the words 'Oon Oom,' and
the language is long since dead in which he speaks, and all
his worshippers are gathered to their tombs, so that none
knoweth what the words portend that he uttereth at dawn.
Some say that he greets the sun as one god greets another
in the language thereof, and others say that he proclaims
the day, and others that he uttereth warning. And at
every gate is a marvel not credible until beholden."

And I gathered three friends and said to them: "We
are what we have seen and known. Let us journey now
and behold Babbulkund, that our minds may be beautified
with it and our spirits made holier."

So we took ship and travelled over the lifting sea, and

remembered not things done in the towns we knew, but laid away the thoughts of them like soiled linen and put them by, and dreamed of Babbulkund.

But when we came to the land of which Babbulkund is the abiding glory, we hired a caravan of camels and Arab guides, and passed southwards in the afternoon on the three days' journey through the desert that should bring us to the white walls of Babbulkund. And the heat of the sun shone upon us out of the bright grey sky, and the heat of the desert beat up at us from below.

About sunset we halted and tethered our horses, while the Arabs unloaded the provisions from the camels and prepared a fire out of the dry scrub, for at sunset the heat of the desert departs from it suddenly, like a bird. Then we saw a traveller approaching us on a camel coming from the south. When he was come near we said to him:

"Come and encamp among us, for in the desert all men are brothers, and we will give thee meat to eat and wine, or, if thou art bound by thy faith, we will give thee some other drink that is not accursed by the prophet."

The traveller seated himself beside us on the sand, and crossed his legs and answered:

"Hearken, and I will tell you of Babbulkund, City of Marvel. Babbulkund stands just below the meeting of the rivers, where Oonrana, River of Myth, flows into the Waters of Fable, even the old stream Plegathanees. These, together, enter her northern gate rejoicing. Of old they flowed in the dark through the Hill that Nehemoth, the first of Pharaohs, carved into the City of Marvel. Sterile and desolate they float far through the desert, each in the appointed cleft, with life upon neither bank, but give birth in Babbulkund to the sacred purple garden whereof all nations sing. Thither all the bees come on a pilgrimage at evening by a secret way of the air. Once, from his twilit kingdom, which he rules equally with the sun, the moon saw and loved Babbulkund, clad with her purple garden;

and the moon wooed Babbulkund, and she sent him weeping away, for she is more beautiful than all her sisters the stars. Her sisters come to her at night into her maiden chamber. Even the gods speak sometimes of Babbulkund, clad with her purple garden. Listen, for I perceive by your eyes that ye have not seen Babbulkund; there is a restlessness in them and an unappeased wonder. Listen. In the garden whereof I spoke there is a lake that hath no twin or fellow in the world; there is no companion for it among all the lakes. The shores of it are of glass, and the bottom of it. In it are great fish having golden and scarlet scales, and they swim to and fro. Here it is the wont of the eighty-second Nehemoth (who rules in the city to-day) to come, after the dusk has fallen, and sit by the lake alone, and at this hour eight hundred slaves go down by steps through caverns into vaults beneath the lake. Four hundred of them carrying purple lights march one behind the other, from east to west, and four hundred carrying green lights march one behind the other, from west to east. The two lines cross and re-cross each other in and out as the slaves go round and round, and the fearful fish flash up and down and to and fro."

But upon that traveller speaking night descended, solemn and cold, and we wrapped ourselves in our blankets and lay down upon the sand in the sight of the astral sisters of Babbulkund. And all that night the desert said many things, softly and in a whisper, but I knew not what he said. Only the sand knew and arose and was troubled and lay down again, and the wind knew. Then, as the hours of the night went by, these two discovered the foot-tracks wherewith we had disturbed the holy desert, and they troubled over them and covered them up; and then the wind lay down and the sand rested. Then the wind arose again and the sand danced. This they did many times. And all the while the desert whispered what I shall not know.

Then I slept awhile and awoke just before sunrise, very cold. Suddenly the sun leapt up and flamed upon our faces; we all threw off our blankets and stood up. Then we took food, and afterwards started southwards, and in the heat of the day rested, and afterwards pushed on again. And all the while the desert remained the same, like a dream that will not cease to trouble a tired sleeper.

And often travellers passed us in the desert, coming from the City of Marvel, and there was a light and a glory in their eyes from having seen Babbulkund.

That evening, at sunset, another traveller neared us, and we hailed him, saying:

"Wilt thou eat and drink with us, seeing that all men are brothers in the desert?"

And he descended from his camel and sat by us and said:

"When morning shines on the colossus Neb and Neb speaks, at once the musicians of King Nehemoth in Babbulkund awake.

"At first their fingers wander over their golden harps, or they stroke idly their violins. Clearer and clearer the note of each instrument ascends like larks arising from the dew, till suddenly they all blend together and a new melody is born. Thus, every morning, the musicians of King Nehemoth make a new marvel in the City of Marvel; for these are no common musicians, but masters of melody, raided by conquest long since, and carried away in ships from the Isles of Song. And, at the sound of the music, Nehemoth awakes in the eastern chamber of his palace, which is carved in the form of a great crescent, four miles long, on the northern side of the city. Full in the windows of its eastern chamber the sun rises, and full in the windows of its western chamber the sun sets.

"When Nehemoth awakes he summons slaves who bring a palanquin with bells, which the King enters, having lightly robed. Then the slaves run and bear him to the onyx Chamber of the Bath, with the sound of small bells ringing as they run. And when Nehemoth emerges thence, bathed and anointed, the slaves run on with their ringing palanquin and bear him to the Orient Chamber of Banquets, where the King takes the first meal of the day. Thence, through the great white corridor whose windows all face sunwards, Nehemoth, in his palanquin, passes on to the Audience Chamber of Embassies from the North, which is all decked with Northern wares.

"All about it are ornaments of amber from the North and carven chalices of the dark brown Northern crystal, and on its floors lie furs from Baltic shores.

"In adjoining chambers are stored the wonted food of the hardy Northern men, and the strong wine of the North, pale but terrible. Therein the King receives barbarian princes from the frigid lands. Thence the slaves bear him swiftly to the Audience Chamber of Embassies from the East, where the walls are of turquoise, studded with the rubies of Ceylon, where the gods are the gods of the East, where all the hangings have been devised in the gorgeous heart of Ind, and where all the carvings have been wrought with the cunning of the isles. Here, if a caravan hath chanced to have come in from Ind or from Cathay, it is the King's wont to converse awhile with Moguls or Mandarins, for from the East come the arts and knowledge of the world, and the converse of their people is polite. Thus Nehemoth passes on through the other Audience Chambers and receives, perhaps, some Sheikhs of the Arab folk who have crossed the great desert from the West, or receives an embassy sent to do him homage from the shy jungle people to the South. And all the while the slaves with the ringing palanquin run westwards, following the sun, and ever the sun shines straight into the chamber where Nehemoth sits, and all the while the music from one or other of his bands of musicians comes tinkling to his ears. But when the middle of the day draws near, the slaves run to the cool groves that lie along the verandahs on the northern side of the palace, forsaking the sun, and as the heat overcomes the genius of the musicians, one by one their hands fall from their instruments, till at last all melody ceases. At this moment Nehemoth falls asleep, and the slaves put the palanquin down and lie down beside it. At this hour the city becomes quite still, and the palace of Nehemoth and the tombs of the Pharaohs of old face to the sunlight, all alike in silence. Even the jewellers in the market-place, selling gems to princes, cease from their bargaining and cease to sing; for in Babbulkund the vendor of rubies sings the song of the ruby, and the vendor of sapphires sings the song of the sapphire, and each stone hath its song, so that a man, by his song, proclaims and makes known his wares.

"But all these sounds cease at the meridian hour, the jewellers in the market-place lie down in what shadow they can find, and the princes go back to the cool places in their palaces, and a great hush in the gleaming air hangs over Babbulkund. But in the cool of the late afternoon, one of the King's musicians will awake from dreaming of his home and will pass his fingers, perhaps, over the strings of his harp and, with the music, some memory may arise of the wind in the glens of the mountains that stand in the Isles of Song. Then the musician will wrench great cries out of the soul of his harp for the sake of the old memory, and his fellows will awake and all make a song of home, woven of sayings told in the harbour when the ships came in, and of tales in the cottages about the people of old time. One by one the other bands of musicians will take up the song, and Babbulkund, City of Marvel, will throb with this marvel anew. Just now Nehemoth awakes, the slaves leap to their feet and bear the palanquin to the outer side of the great crescent palace between the south and the west, to behold the sun again. The palanquin, with its ringing bells, goes round once more; the voices of the jewellers sing again, in the market-place, the song of the emerald, the song of the sapphire; men talk on the housetops, beggars wail in the streets, the musicians bend to their work, all the sounds blend together into one murmur, the voice of Babbulkund speaking at evening. Lower and lower sinks the sun, till Nehemoth, following it, comes with his panting slaves to the great purple garden of which surely thine own country has its songs, from wherever thou art come.

"There he alights from his palanquin and goes up to a throne of ivory set in the garden's midst, facing full westwards, and sits there alone, long regarding the sunlight until it is quite gone. At this hour trouble comes into the face of Nehemoth. Men have heard him muttering at the time of sunset: 'Even I too, even I too.' Thus do King Nehemoth and the sun make their glorious ambits about Babbulkund.

"A little later, when the stars come out to envy the beauty of the City of Marvel, the King walks to another part of the garden and sits in an alcove of opal all alone by the marge of the sacred lake. This is the lake whose shores and floors are of glass, which is lit from beneath by slaves with purple lights and with green lights intermingling, and is one of the seven wonders of Babbulkund. Three of the wonders are in the city's midst and four are at her gates. There is the lake, of which I tell thee, and the purple garden of which I have told thee and which is a wonder even to the stars, and there is Ong Zwarba, of which I shall tell thee also. And the wonders at the gates are these. At the eastern gate Neb. And at the northern gate the wonder of the river and the arches, for the River of Myth, which becomes one with the Waters of Fable in the desert outside the city, floats under a gate of pure gold, rejoicing, and under many arches fantastically carven that are one with either bank. The marvel at the western gate is the marvel of Annolith and the dog Voth. Annolith sits outside the western gate facing towards the city. He is higher than any of the towers or palaces, for his head was carved from the summit of the old hill; he hath two eyes of sapphire wherewith he regards Babbulkund, and the wonder of the eyes is that they are to-day in the same sockets wherein they glowed when first the world began, only the marble that covered them has been carven away and the light of day let in and the sight of the envious stars. Larger than a lion is the dog Voth beside him; every hair is carven upon the back of Voth, his war hackles are erected and his teeth are bared. All the Nehemoths have worshipped the god Annolith, but all their people pray to the dog Voth, for the law of the land is that none but a Nehemoth may worship the god Annolith. The marvel at the southern gate is the marvel of the jungle, for he comes with all his wild un-travelled sea of darkness and trees and tigers and sunward-aspiring orchids right through a marble gate in the city wall and enters the city, and there widens and holds a space in its midst of many miles across. Moreover, he is older than the City of Marvel, for he dwelt long since in one of the valleys of the mountain which Nehemoth, first of Pharaohs, carved into Babbulkund.

"Now the opal alcove in which the King sits at evening by the lake stands at the edge of the jungle, and the climbing orchids of the jungle have long since crept from their homes through clefts of the opal alcove, lured by the lights of the lake, and now bloom there exultingly. Near to this alcove are the harems of Nehemoth.

"The King hath four harems—one for the stalwart women from the mountains to the north, one for the dark and furtive jungle women, one for the desert women that have wandering souls and pine in Babbulkund, and one for the princesses of his own kith, whose brown cheeks blush with the blood of ancient Pharaohs and who exult with Babbulkund in her surpassing beauty, and who know nought of the desert or the jungle or the bleak hills to the north. Quite unadorned and clad in simple garments go all the kith of Nehemoth, for they know well that he grows weary of pomp. Unadorned all save one, the Princess Linderith,

who weareth Ong Zwarba and the three lesser gems of the
sea. Such a stone is Ong Zwarba that there are none like
it even in the turban of Nehemoth nor in all the sanctuaries
of the sea. The same god that made Linderith made long
ago Ong Zwarba; she and Ong Zwarba shine together with
one light, and beside this marvellous stone gleam the three
lesser ones of the sea.

"Now when the King sitteth in his opal alcove by the
sacred lake with the orchids blooming around him all sounds
are become still. The sound of the tramping of the weary
slaves as they go round and round never comes to the surface. Long since the musicians sleep, and their hands have
fallen dumb upon their instruments, and the voices in the
city have died away. Perhaps a sigh of one of the desert
women has become half a song, or on a hot night in summer
one of the women of the hills sings softly a song of snow;
all night long in the midst of the purple garden sings one
nightingale; all else is still; the stars that look on Babbulkund arise and set, the cold unhappy moon drifts lonely
through them, the night wears on; at last the dark figure of
Nehemoth, eighty-second of his line, rises and moves stealthily away."

The traveller ceased to speak. For a long time the clear
stars, sisters of Babbulkund, had shone upon him speaking,
the desert wind had arisen and whispered to the sand, and
the sand had long gone secretly to and fro; none of us had
moved, none of us had fallen asleep, not so much from
wonder at his tale as from the thought that we ourselves
in two days' time should see that wondrous city. Then we
wrapped our blankets around us and lay down with our
feet towards the embers of our fire and instantly were
asleep, and in our dreams we multiplied the fame of the
City of Marvel.

The sun arose and flamed upon our faces, and all the
desert glinted with its light. Then we stood up and prepared the morning meal, and, when we had eaten, the

traveller departed. And we commended his soul to the god of the land whereto he went, of the land of his home to the northward, and he commended our souls to the God of the people of the land where from we had come. Then a traveller overtook us going on foot; he wore a brown cloak that was all in rags and he seemed to have been walking all night, and he walked hurriedly but appeared weary, so we offered him food and drink, of which he partook thankfully. When we asked him where he was going, he answered "Babbulkund." Then we offered him a camel upon which to ride, for we said, "We also go to Babbulkund," But he answered strangely:

"Nay, pass on before me, for it is a sore thing never to have seen Babbulkund, having lived while yet she stood. Pass on before me and behold her, and then flee away at once, returning northward."

Then, though we understood him not, we left him, for he was insistent, and passed on our journey southwards through the desert, and we came before the middle of the day to an oasis of palm trees standing by a well and there we gave water to the haughty camels and replenished our water-bottles and soothed our eyes with the sight of green things and tarried for many hours in the shade. Some of the men slept, but of those that remained awake each man sang softly the songs of his own country, telling of Babbulkund. When the afternoon was far spent we travelled a little way southwards, and went on through the cool evening until the sun fell low and we encamped, and as we sat in our encampment the man in rags overtook us, having travelled all the day, and we gave him food and drink again, and in the twilight he spoke, saying:

"I am the servant of the Lord the God of my people, and I go to do his work on Babbulkund. She is the most beautiful city in the world; there hath been none like her, even the stars of God go envious of her beauty. She is all white, yet with streaks of pink that pass through her streets

and houses like flames in the white mind of a sculptor, like
desire in Paradise. She hath been carved of old out of a
holy hill, no slaves wrought the City of Marvel, but artists
toiling at the work they loved. They took no pattern from
the houses of men, but each man wrought what his inner
eye had seen and carved in marble the visions of his dream.
All over the roof of one of the palace chambers winged lions
flit like bats, the size of every one is the size of the lions of
God, and the wings are larger than any wing created; they
are one above the other more than a man can number, they
are all carven out of one block of marble, the chamber itself
is hollowed from it, and it is borne aloft upon the carven
branches of a grove of clustered tree-ferns wrought by the
hand of some jungle mason that loved the tall fern well.
Over the River of Myth, which is one with the Waters of
Fable, go bridges, fashioned like the wisteria tree and like
the drooping laburnum, and a hundred others of wonderful
devices, the desire of the souls of masons a long while dead.
Oh! very beautiful is white Babbulkund, very beautiful she
is, but proud; and the Lord the God of my people hath
seen her in her pride, and looking towards her hath seen the
prayers of Nehemoth going up to the abomination Annolith,
and all the people following after Voth. She is very beautiful, Babbulkund; alas, that I may not bless her. I could
live always on one of her inner terraces looking on the mysterious jungle in her midst and the heavenward faces of the
orchids that, clambering from the darkness, behold the sun.
I could love Babbulkund with a great love, yet am I the
servant of the Lord the God of my people, and the King
hath sinned unto the abomination Annolith, and the people
lust exceedingly for Voth. Alas for thee, Babbulkund,
alas that I may not even now turn back, for to-morrow I
must prophesy against thee and cry out against thee, Babbulkund. But ye travellers that have entreated me hos-
pitably, rise and pass on with your camels, for I can tarry
no longer, and I go to do the work on Babbulkund of the

Lord the God of my people. Go now and see the beauty of Babbulkund before I cry out against her, and then flee swiftly northwards."

A smouldering fragment fell in upon our camp fire and sent a strange light into the eyes of the man in rags. He rose at once, and his tattered cloak swirled up with him like a great wing; he said no more, but turned round from us instantly southwards, and strode away into the darkness towards Babbulkund. Then a hush fell upon our encampment, and the smell of the tobacco of those lands arose. When the last flame died down in our camp fire I fell asleep, but my rest was troubled by shifting dreams of doom.

Morning came, and our guides told us that we should come to the city ere nightfall. Again we passed southwards through the changeless desert; sometimes we met travellers coming from Babbulkund, with the beauty of its marvels still fresh in their eyes.

When we encamped near the middle of the day we saw a great number of people on foot coming towards us running, from the southwards. These we hailed when they were come near, saying, "What of Babbulkund?"

They answered: "We are not of the race of the people of Babbulkund, but were captured in youth and taken away from the hills that are to the northward. Now we have all seen in visions of the stillness the Lord the God of our people calling to us from His hills, and therefore we all flee northward. But in Babbulkund King Nehemoth hath been troubled in the nights by unkingly dreams of doom, and none may interpret what the dreams portend. Now this is the dream that King Nehemoth dreamed on the first night of his dreaming. He saw move through the stillness a bird all black, and beneath the beatings of his wings Babbulkund gloomed and darkened; and after him flew a bird all white, beneath the beatings of whose wings Babbulkund gleamed and shone; and there flew by four more birds alternately black and white. And, as the black ones passed Babbulkund darkened, and when the white ones appeared her streets and houses shone. But after the sixth bird there came no more, and Babbulkund vanished from her place, and there was only the empty desert where she had stood, and the rivers Onrana and Plegáthanees mourning alone. Next morning all the prophets of the King gathered before their abominations and questioned them of the dream, and the abominations spake not. But when the second night stepped down from the halls of God, dowered with many stars, King Nehemoth dreamed again; and in this dream King Nehemoth saw four birds only, black, and white alternately as before. And Babbulkund darkened again as the black ones passed, and shone when the white came by; only after the four birds came no more, and Babbulkund vanished from her place, leaving only the forgetful desert and the mourning rivers.

"Still the abominations spake not, and none could interpret the dream. And when the third night came forth from the divine halls of her home dowered like her sisters, again King Nehemoth dreamed. And he saw a bird all black go by again, beneath whom Babbulkund darkened, and then a white bird and Babbulkund shone; and after them came no more, and Babbulkund passed away. And the golden day appeared, dispelling dreams, and still the abominations were silent, and the King's prophets answered not to portend the omen of the dream. One prophet only spake before the King, saying: 'The sable birds, O King, are the nights, and the white birds are the days, . . .' This thing the King had feared, and he arose and smote the prophet with his sword, whose soul went crying away and had to do no more with nights and days.

"It was last night that the King dreamed his third dream, and this morning we fled away from Babbulkund. A great heat lies over it, and the orchids of the jungle droop their heads. All night long the women in the harem of the North have wailed horribly for their hills. A fear hath fallen upon the city, and a boding. Twice hath Nehemoth gone to worship Annolith, and all the people have prostrated themselves before Voth. Thrice the horologers have looked into the great crystal globe wherein are foretold all happenings to be, and thrice the globe was blank. Yea, though they went a fourth time yet was no vision revealed; and the people's voice is hushed in Babbulkund."

Soon the travellers arose and pushed on northwards again, leaving us wondering. Through the heat of the day we rested as well as we might, but the air was motionless and sultry and the camels ill at ease. The Arabs said that it boded a desert storm, and that a great wind would arise full of sand. So we arose in the afternoon, and travelled swiftly, hoping to come to shelter before the storm. And the air burned in the stillness between the baked desert and the glaring sky.

Suddenly a wind arose out of the South, blowing from Babbulkund, and the sand lifted and went by in great shapes, all whispering. And the wind blew violently, and wailed as it blew, and hundreds of sandy shapes went towering by, and there were little cries among them and the sounds of a passing away. Soon the wind sank quite suddenly, and its cries died, and the panic ceased among the driven sands. And when the storm departed the air was cool, and the terrible sultriness and the boding were passed away, and the camels had ease among them. And the Arabs said that the storm which was to be had been, as was willed of old by God.

The sun set and the gloaming came, and we neared the junction of Oonrana and Plegáthanees, but in the darkness discerned not Babbulkund. We pushed on hurriedly to reach the city ere nightfall, and came to the junction of the River of Myth where he meets with the Waters of Fable, and still saw not Babbulkund. All round us lay the sand and rocks of the unchanging desert, save to the southwards where the jungle stood with its orchids facing skywards.

Then we perceived that we had arrived too late, and that her doom had come to Babbulkund; and by the river in the empty desert on the sand the man in rags was seated, with his face hidden in his hands, weeping bitterly.

·　　·　　·　　·　　·　　·　　·　　·

Thus passed away in the hour of her iniquities before Annolith, in the two thousand and thirty-second year of her being, in the six thousand and fiftieth year of the building of the World, Babbulkund, City of Marvel, sometime called by those that hated her City of the Dog, but hourly mourned in Araby and Ind and wide through jungle and desert; leaving no memorial in stone to show that she had been, but remembered with an abiding love, in spite of the anger of God, by all that knew her beauty, whereof still they sing.

THE KITH OF THE ELF-FOLK

CHAPTER I

THE north wind was blowing, and red and golden the last days of Autumn were streaming hence. Solemn and cold over the marshes arose the evening.

It became very still.

Then the last pigeon went home to the trees on the dry land in the distance, whose shapes already had taken upon themselves a mystery in the haze.

Then all was still again.

As the light faded and the haze deepened, mystery crept nearer from every side.

Then the green plover came in crying, and all alighted.

And again it became still, save when one of the plover arose and flew a little way uttering the cry of the waste. And hushed and silent became the earth, expecting the first star. Then the duck came in, and the widgeon, company by company: and all the light of day faded out of the sky saving one red band of light. Across the light appeared, black and huge, the wings of a flock of geese beating up wind to the marshes. These, too, went down among the rushes.

Then the stars appeared and shone in the stillness, and there was silence in the great spaces of the night.

Suddenly the bells of the cathedral in the marshes broke out, calling to evensong.

Eight centuries ago on the edge of the marsh men had built the huge cathedral, or it may have been seven centuries ago, or perhaps nine—it was all one to the Wild things.

So evensong was held, and candles lighted, and the lights through the windows shone red and green in the water, and the sound of the organ went roaring over the marshes. But from the deep and perilous places, edged with bright mosses, the Wild Things came leaping up to dance on the reflection of the stars, and over their heads as they danced the marsh-lights rose and fell.

The Wild Things are somewhat human in appearance, only all brown of skin and barely two feet high. Their ears are pointed like the squirrel's, only far larger, and they leap to prodigious heights. They live all day under deep pools in the loneliest marshes, but at night they come up and dance. Each Wild Thing has over its head a marsh-light, which moves as the Wild Thing moves; they have no souls, and cannot die, and are of the kith of the Elf-folk.

All night they dance over the marshes treading upon the reflection of the stars (for the bare surface of the water will not hold them by itself); but when the stars begin to pale, they sink down one by one into the pools of their home. Or if they tarry longer, sitting upon the rushes, their bodies fade from view as the marsh-fires pale in the light, and by daylight none may see the Wild Things of the kith of the Elf-folk. Neither may any see them even at night unless they were born, as I was, in the hour of dusk, just at the moment when the first star appears.

Now, on the night that I tell of, a little Wild Thing had gone drifting over the waste, till it came right up to the walls of the cathedral and danced upon the images of the coloured saints as they lay in the water among the reflection of the stars. And as it leaped in its fantastic dance, it saw through the painted windows to where the people prayed, and heard the organ roaring over the marshes.

The sound of the organ roared over the marshes, but the song and prayers of the people streamed up from the cathedral's highest tower like thin gold chains, and reached to Paradise, and up and down them went the angels from Paradise to the people, and from the people to Paradise again.

Then something akin to discontent troubled the Wild Thing for the first time since the making of the marshes; and the soft grey ooze and the chill of the deep water seemed to be not enough, nor the first arrival from northwards of the tumultuous geese, nor the wild rejoicing of the wings of the wildfowl when every feather sings, nor the wonder of the calm ice that comes when the snipe depart and beards the rushes with frost and clothes the hushed waste with a mysterious haze where the sun goes red and low, nor even the dance of the Wild Things in the marvellous night; and the little Wild Thing longed to have a soul, and to go and worship God.

And when evensong was over and the lights were out, it went back crying to its kith.

But on the next night, as soon as the images of the stars appeared in the water, it went leaping away from star to star to the farthest edge of the marshlands, where a great wood grew where dwelt the Oldest of the Wild Things.

And it found the Oldest of Wild Things sitting under a tree, sheltering itself from the moon.

And the little Wild Thing said: "I want to have a soul to worship God, and to know the meaning of music, and to see the inner beauty of the marshlands and to imagine Paradise."

And the Oldest of the Wild Things said to it: "What have we to do with God? We are only Wild Things, and of the kith of the Elf-folk."

But it only answered, "I want to have a soul."

Then the Oldest of the Wild Things said: "I have no soul to give you; but if you got a soul, one day you would have to die, and if you knew the meaning of music you would learn the meaning of sorrow, and it is better to be a Wild Thing and not to die."

So it went weeping away.

But they that were kin to the Elf-folk were sorry for the little Wild Thing; and though the Wild Things cannot sorrow long, having no souls to sorrow with, yet they felt for awhile a soreness where their souls should be when they saw the grief of their comrade.

So the kith of the Elf-folk went abroad by night to make a soul for the little Wild Thing. And they went over the marshes till they came to the high fields among the flowers and grasses. And there they gathered a large piece of gossamer that the spider had laid by twilight; and the dew was on it.

Into this dew had shone all the lights of the long banks of the ribbed sky, as all the colours changed in the restful spaces of evening. And over it the marvellous night had gleamed with all its stars.

Then the Wild Things went with their dew-bespangled gossamer down to the edge of their home. And there they gathered a piece of the grey mist that lies by night over the marshlands. And into it they put the melody of the waste that is borne up and down the marshes in the evening on the wings of the golden plover. And they put into it, too, the mournful songs that the reeds are compelled to sing before the presence of the arrogant North Wind. Then each of the Wild Things gave some treasured memory of the old marshes, "For we can spare it," they said. And to all this they added a few images of the stars that they gathered out of the water. Still the soul that the kith of the Elf-folk were making had no life.

Then they put into it the low voices of two lovers that went walking in the night, wandering late alone. And after that they waited for the dawn. And the queenly dawn appeared, and the marsh-lights of the Wild Things paled in the glare, and their bodies faded from view; and still they waited by the marsh's edge. And to them waiting came over field and marsh, from the ground and out of the sky, the myriad song of the birds.

This, too, the Wild Things put into the piece of haze that they had gathered in the marshlands, and wrapped it all up in their dew-bespangled gossamer. Then the soul lived.

And there it lay in the hands of the Wild Things no larger than a hedgehog; and wonderful lights were in it, green and blue; and they changed ceaselessly, going round and round, and in the grey midst of it was a purple flare.

And the next night they came to the little Wild Thing and showed her the gleaming soul. And they said to her: "If you must have a soul and go and worship God, and become a mortal and die, place this to your left breast a little above the heart, and it will enter and you will become a human. But if you take it you can never be rid of it to become a mortal again unless you pluck it out and give it to another; and *we* will not take it, and most of the humans have a soul already. And if you cannot find a human without a soul you will one day die, and your soul cannot go to Paradise because it was only made in the marshes."

Far away the little Wild Thing saw the cathedral windows alight for evensong, and the song of the people mounting up to Paradise, and all the angels going up and down. So it bid farewell with tears and thanks to the Wild Things of the Kith of Elf-folk, and went leaping away towards the green dry land, holding the soul in its hands.

And the Wild Things were sorry that it had gone, but could not be sorry long because they had no souls.

At the marsh's edge the little Wild Thing gazed for some moments over the water to where the marsh-fires were leaping up and down, and then pressed the soul against its left breast a little above the heart.

Instantly it became a young and beautiful woman, who was cold and frightened. She clad herself somehow with bundles of reeds, and went towards the lights of a house that stood close by. And she pushed open the door and entered, and found a farmer and a farmer's wife sitting over their supper.

And the farmer's wife took the little Wild Thing with the soul of the marshes up to her room, and clothed her and braided her hair, and brought her down again, and gave her the first food that she had ever eaten. Then the farmer's wife asked many questions.

"Where have you come from?" she said.

"Over the marshes."

"From what direction?" said the farmer's wife.

"South," said the little Wild Thing with the new soul.

"But none can come over the marshes from the south " said the farmer's wife.

"No, they can't do that," said the farmer.

"I lived in the marshes."

"Who are you?" asked the farmer's wife.

"I am a Wild Thing, and have found a soul in the marshes, and we are kin to the Elf-folk."

Talking it over afterwards, the farmer and his wife agreed that she must be a gipsy who had been lost, and that she was queer with hunger and exposure.

So that night the little Wild Thing slept in the farmer's house, but her new soul stayed awake the whole night long dreaming of the beauty of the marshes.

As soon as dawn came over the waste and shone on the farmer's house, she looked from the window towards the glittering waters, and saw the inner beauty of the marsh. For the Wild Things only love the marsh and know its haunts, but now she perceived the mystery of its distances and the glamour of its perilous pools, with their fair and deadly mosses, and felt the marvel of the North Wind who comes dominant out of unknown icy lands, and the wonder of that ebb and flow of life when the wildfowl whirl in at evening to the marshlands and at dawn pass out to sea. And she knew that over her head above the farmer's house

stretched wide Paradise, where perhaps God was now imag-
ining a sunrise while angels played low on lutes, and the
sun came rising up on the world below to gladden fields
and marshes.

And all that heaven thought, the marsh thought too; for
the blue of the marsh was as the blue of heaven, and the
great cloud shapes in heaven became the shapes in the
marsh, and through each ran momentary rivers of purple,
errant between banks of gold. And the stalwart army of
reeds appeared out of the gloom with all their pennons
waving as far as the eye could see. And from another
window she saw the vast cathedral gathering its ponder-
ous strength together, and lifting it up in towers out of
the marshlands.

She said, "I will never, never leave the marsh."

An hour later she dressed with great difficulty and went
down to eat the second meal of her life. The farmer and
his wife were kindly folk, and taught her how to eat.

"I suppose the gipsies don't have knives and forks," one
said to the other afterwards.

After breakfast the farmer went and saw the Dean, who
lived near his cathedral, and presently returned and brought
back to the Dean's house the little Wild Thing with the
new soul.

"This is the lady," said the farmer. "This is Dean
Murnith." Then he went away.

"Ah," said the Dean, "I understand you were lost the
other night in the marshes. It was a terrible night to be
lost in the marshes.

"I love the marshes," said the little Wild Thing with the
new soul.

"Indeed! How old are you?" said the Dean.

"I don't know," she answered.

"You must know about how old you are," he said.

"Oh, about ninety," she said, "or more."

"Ninety years!" exclaimed the Dean.

"No, ninety centuries," she said; "I am as old as the marshes."

Then she told her story—how she had longed to be a human and go and worship God, and have a soul and see the beauty of the world, and how all the Wild Things had made her a soul of gossamer and mist and music and strange memories.

"But if this is true," said Dean Murnith, "this is very wrong. God cannot have intended you to have a soul. What is your name?"

"I have no name," she answered.

"We must find a Christian name and a surname for you. What would you like to be called?"

"Song of the Rushes," she said.

"That won't do at all," said the Dean.

"Then I would like to be called Terrible North Wind, or Star in the Waters," she said.

"No, no, no," said Dean Murnith; "that is quite impossible. We could call you Miss Rush if you like. How would Mary Rush do? Perhaps you had better have another name—say Mary Jane Rush."

So the little Wild Thing with the soul of the marshes took the names that were offered her, and became Mary Jane Rush.

"And we must find something for you to do," said Dean Murnith. "Meanwhile we can give you a room here."

"I don't want to do anything," replied Mary Jane; "I want to worship God in the cathedral and live beside the marshes."

Then Mrs. Murnith came in, and for the rest of that day Mary Jane stayed at the house of the Dean.

And there with her new soul she perceived the beauty of the world; for it came grey and level out of misty distances, and widened into grassy fields and ploughlands right up to the edge of an old gabled town; and solitary in the fields far off an ancient windmill stood, and his honest hand-made sails went round and round in the free East Anglian winds. Close by, the gabled houses leaned out over the streets, planted fair upon sturdy timbers that grew in the olden time, all glorying among themselves upon their beauty. And out of them, buttress by buttress, growing and going upwards, aspiring tower by tower, rose the cathedral.

And she saw the people moving in the streets all leisurely and slow, and unseen among them, whispering to each other, unheard by living men and concerned only with bygone things, drifted the ghosts of very long ago. And wherever the streets ran eastwards, wherever were gaps in the houses, always there broke into view the sight of the great marshes, like to some bar of music weird and strange that haunts a melody, arising again and again, played on the violin by one musician only, who plays no other bar, and he is swart and lank about the hair and bearded about the lips, and his moustache droops long and low, and no one knows the land from which he comes.

All these were good things for a new soul to see.

Then the sun set over green fields and ploughlands and the night came up. One by one the merry lights of cheery lamp-lit windows took their stations in the solemn night.

Then the bells rang, far up in a cathedral tower, and their melody fell on the roofs of the old houses and poured over their eaves until the streets were full, and then flooded away over green fields and ploughlands till it came to the sturdy mill and brought the miller trudging to evensong, and far away eastwards and seawards the sound rang out over the remoter marshes. And it was all as yesterday to the old ghosts in the streets.

Then the Dean's wife took Mary Jane to evening service, and she saw three hundred candles filling all the aisle with light. But sturdy pillars stood there in unlit vastnesses; great colonnades going away into the gloom where evening and morning, year in year out, they did their work in the dark, holding the cathedral roof aloft. And it was stiller than the marshes are still when the ice has come and the wind that brought it has fallen.

Suddenly into this stillness rushed the sound of the organ, roaring, and presently the people prayed and sang.

No longer could Mary Jane see their prayers ascending like thin gold chains, for that was but an elfin fancy, but she imagined clear in her new soul the seraphs passing in the ways of Paradise, and the angels changing guard to watch the World by night.

When the Dean had finished service, a young curate, Mr. Millings, went up into the pulpit.

He spoke of Abana and Pharpar, rivers of Damascus: and Mary Jane was glad that there were rivers having such names, and heard with wonder of Nineveh, that great city, and many things strange and new.

And the light of the candles shone on the curate's fair hair, and his voice went ringing down the aisle, and Mary Jane rejoiced that he was there.

But when his voice stopped she felt a sudden loneliness, such as she had not felt since the making of the marshes; for the Wild Things never are lonely and never unhappy, but dance all night on the reflection of the stars, and having no souls desire nothing more.

After the collection was made, before any one moved to go, Mary Jane walked up the aisle to Mr. Millings.

"I love you," she said.

_____

CHAPTER II

Nobody sympathised with Mary Jane. "So unfortunate for Mr. Millings," every one said; "such a promising young man."

Mary Jane was sent away to a great manufacturing city of the Midlands, where work had been found for her in a cloth factory. And there was nothing in that town that was good for a soul to see. For it did not know that beauty was to be desired; so it made many things by machinery, and became hurried in all its ways, and boasted its superiority over other cities and became richer and richer, and there was none to pity it.

In this city Mary Jane had had lodgings found for her near the factory.

At six o'clock on those November mornings, about the time that, far away from the city, the wildfowl rose up out of the calm marshes and passed to the troubled spaces of the sea, at six o'clock the factory uttered a prolonged howl and gathered the workers together, and there they worked, saving two hours for food, the whole of the daylit hours and into the dark till the bells tolled six again.

There Mary Jane worked with other girls in a long dreary room, where giants sat pounding wool into a long thread-like strip with iron, rasping hands. And all day long they roared as they sat at their soulless work. But the work of Mary Jane was not with these, only their roar was ever in her ears as their clattering iron limbs went to and fro.

Her work was to tend a creature smaller, but infinitely more cunning.

It took the strip of wool that the giants had threshed, and whirled it round and round until it had twisted it into hard thin thread. Then it would make a clutch with fingers of steel at the thread that it had gathered, and waddle away about five yards and come back with more.

It had mastered all the subtlety of skilled workers, and had gradually displaced them; one thing only it could not do, it was unable to pick up the ends if a piece of the thread broke, in order to tie them together again. For this a human soul was required, and it was Mary Jane's business to pick up broken ends; and the moment she placed them together the busy soulless creature tied them for itself.

All here was ugly; even the green wool as it whirled round and round was neither the green of the grass nor yet the green of the rushes, but a sorry muddy green that befitted a sullen city under a murky sky.

When she looked out over the roofs of the town, there too was ugliness; and well the houses knew it, for with hideous stucco they aped in grotesque mimicry the pillars and temples of old Greece, pretending to one another to be that which they were not. And emerging from these houses and going in, and seeing the pretence of paint and stucco year after year until it all peeled away, the souls of the poor owners of those houses sought to be other souls until they grew weary of it.

At evening Mary Jane went back to her lodgings. Only then, after the dark had fallen, could the soul of Mary Jane perceive any beauty in that city, when the lamps were lit and here and there a star shone through the smoke. Then she would have gone abroad and beheld the night, but this the old woman to whom she was confided would not let her do. And the days multiplied themselves by seven and became weeks, and the weeks passed by, and all days were the same. And all the while the soul of Mary Jane was crying for beautiful things, and found not one, saving on Sundays, when she went to church, and left it to find the city greyer than before.

One day she decided that it was better to be a Wild Thing in the lonely marshes than to have a soul that cried for beautiful things and found not one. From that day she determined to be rid of her soul, so she told her story to one of the factory girls, and said to her:

"The other girls are poorly clad and they do soulless work; surely some of them have no souls and would take mine."

But the factory girl said to her: "All the poor have souls. It is all they have."

Then Mary Jane watched the rich whenever she saw

them, and vainly sought for some one without a soul.

One day at the hour when the machines rested and the human beings that tended them rested too, the wind being at that time from the direction of the marshlands, the soul of Mary Jane lamented bitterly. Then, as she stood outside the factory gates, the soul irresistibly compelled her to sing, and a wild song came from her lips hymning the marshlands. And into her song came crying her yearning for home and for the sound of the shout of the North Wind, masterful and proud, with his lovely lady the snow; and she sang of tales that the rushes murmured to one another, tales that the teal knew and the watchful heron. And over the crowded streets her song went crying away, the song of waste places and of wild free lands, full of wonder and magic, for she had in her elf-made soul the song of the birds and the roar of the organ in the marshes.

At this moment Signor Thompsoni, the well-known English tenor, happened to go by with a friend. They stopped and listened; every one stopped and listened.

"There has been nothing like this in Europe in my time," said Signor Thompsoni.

So a change came into the life of Mary Jane.

People were written to, and finally it was arranged that she should take a leading part in the Covent Garden Opera in a few weeks.

So she went to London to learn.

London and singing lessons were better than the City of the Midlands and those terrible machines. Yet still Mary Jane was not free to go and live as she liked by the edge of the marshlands, and she was still determined to be rid of her soul, but could find no one that had not a soul of their own.

One day she was told that the English people would not listen to her as Miss Rush, and was asked what more suitable name she would like to be called by.

"I would like to be called Terrible North Wind," said Mary Jane, "or Song of the Rushes."

When she was told that this was impossible and Signorina Maria Russiano was suggested, she acquiesced at once, as she had acquiesced when they took her away from her curate; she knew nothing of the ways of humans.

At last the day of the Opera came round, and it was a cold day of the winter.

And Signorina Russiano appeared on the stage before a crowded house.

And Signorina Russiano sang.

And into the song went all the longing of her soul, the soul that could not go to Paradise, but could only worship God and know the meaning of music, and the longing pervaded that Italian song as the infinite mystery of the hills is borne along the sound of distant sheep-bells. Then in the souls that were in that crowded house arose little memories of a great while since that were quite, quite dead, and lived awile again during that marvellous song.

And a strange chill went into the blood of all that listened, as though they stood on the border of bleak marshes and the North Wind blew.

And some it moved to sorrow and some to regret, and some to an unearthly joy,— then suddenly the song went wailing away like the winds of the winter from the marshlands when Spring appears from the South.

So it ended. And a great silence fell fog like over all that house, breaking in upon the end of a chatty conversation that Celia, Countess of Birmingham, was enjoying with a friend.

In the dead hush Signorina Russiano rushed from the stage; she appeared again running among the audience, and dashed up to Lady Birmingham.

"Take my soul," she said; "it is a beautiful soul. It can worship God, and knows the meaning of music and can imagine Paradise. And if you go to the marshlands with it you will see beautiful things; there is an old town there built of lovely timbers, with ghosts in its streets."

Lady Birmingham stared. Every one was standing up. "See," said Signorina Russiano, "it is a beautiful soul."

And she clutched at her left breast a little above the heart, and there was the soul shining in her hand, with the green and blue lights going round and round and the purple flare in the midst.

"Take it," she said, "and you will love all that is beautiful, and know the four winds, each one by his name, and the songs of the birds at dawn. I do not want it, because I am not free. Put it to your left breast a little above the heart."

Still everybody was standing up, and Lady Birmingham felt uncomfortable.

"Please offer it to some one else," she said.

"But they all have souls already," said Signorina Russiano. And everybody went on standing up. And Lady Birmingham took the soul in her hand.

"Perhaps it is lucky," she said.

She felt that she wanted to pray.

She half-closed her eyes, and said "Unberufen." Then she put the soul to her left breast a little above the heart, and hoped that the people would sit down and the singer go away.

Instantly a heap of clothes collapsed before her. For a moment, in the shadow among the seats, those who were born in the dusk hour might have seen a little brown thing leaping free from the clothes, then it sprang into the bright light of the hall, and became invisible to any human eye.

It dashed about for a little, then found the door, and presently was in the lamplit streets.

To those that were born in the dusk hour it might have been seen leaping rapidly wherever the streets ran northwards and eastwards, disappearing from human sight as

it passed under the lamps and appearing again beyond them
with a marsh-light over its head.

Once a dog perceived it and gave chase, and was left
far behind.

The cats of London, who are all born in the dusk hour,
howled fearfully as it went by.

Presently it came to the meaner streets, where the houses
are smaller. Then it went due north-eastwards, leaping
from roof to roof. And so in a few minutes it came to
more open spaces, and then to the desolate lands, where
market gardens grow, which are neither town nor country.
Till at last the good black trees came into view, with their
demoniac shapes in the night, and the grass was cold and wet,
and the night-mist floated over it. And a great white owl
came by, going up and down in the dark. And at all these
things the little Wild Thing rejoiced elvishly.

And it left London far behind it, reddening the sky,
and could distinguish no longer its unlovely roar, but heard
again the noises of the night.

And now it would come through a hamlet glowing and
comfortable in the night; and now to the dark, wet, open
fields again; and many an owl it overtook as they drifted
through the night, a people friendly to the Elf-folk. Sometimes it crossed wide rivers, leaping from star to star; and,
choosing its way as it went, to avoid the hard rough roads,
came before midnight to the East Anglian lands.

And it heard there the shout of the North Wind, who
was dominant and angry, as he drove southwards his adventurous geese; while the rushes bent before him chaunting
plaintively and low, like enslaved rowers of some fabulous
trireme, bending and swinging under blows of the lash, and
singing all the while a doleful song.

And it felt the good dank air that clothes by night the
broad East Anglian lands, and came again to some old
perilous pool where the soft green mosses grew, and there
plunged downward and downward into the dear dark water

till it felt the homely ooze once more coming up between its toes. Thence, out of the lovely chill that is in the heart of the ooze, it arose renewed and rejoicing to dance upon the image of the stars.

I chanced to stand that night by the marsh's edge, forgetting in my mind the affairs of men; and I saw the marsh-fires come leaping up from all the perilous places. And they came up by flocks the whole night long to the number of a great multitude, and danced away together over the marshes.

And I believe that there was a great rejoicing all that night among the kith of the Elf-folk.

THE HIGHWAYMAN

TOM O' THE ROADS had ridden his last ride, and was now alone in the night. From where he was, a man might see the white recumbent sheep and the black outline of the lonely downs, and the grey line of the farther and lonelier downs beyond them; or in hollows far below him, out of the pitiless wind, he might see the grey smoke of hamlets arising from black valleys. But all alike was black to the eyes of Tom, and all the sounds were silence in his ears; only his soul struggled to slip from the iron chains and to pass southwards into Paradise. And the wind blew and blew.

For Tom to-night had nought but the wind to ride; they had taken his true black horse on the day when they took from him the green fields and the sky, men's voices and the laughter of women, and had left him alone with chains about his neck to swing in the wind for ever. And the wind blew and blew.

But the soul of Tom o' the Roads was nipped by the cruel chains, and whenever it struggled to escape it was beaten backwards into the iron collar by the wind that blows from Paradise from the south. And swinging there by the neck, there fell away old sneers from off his lips, and scoffs that he had long since scoffed at God fell from his tongue, and there rotted old bad lusts out of his heart, and from his fingers the stains of deeds that were evil; and they all fell to the ground and grew there in pallid rings and clusters. And when these ill things had all fallen away, Tom's soul was clean again, as his early love had found it, a long while since in spring; and it swung up there in the wind with the bones of Tom, and with his old torn coat and rusty chains.

And the wind blew and blew.

And ever and anon the souls of the sepulchred, coming from consecrated acres, would go by beating up wind to Paradise past the Gallows Tree and past the soul of Tom, that might not go free.

Night after night Tom watched the sheep upon the downs with empty hollow sockets, till his dead hair grew and covered his poor dead face, and hid the shame of it from the sheep. And the wind blew and blew.

Sometimes on gusts of the wind came some one's tears, and beat and beat against the iron chains, but could not rust them through. And the wind blew and blew.

And every evening all the thoughts that Tom had ever uttered came flocking in from doing their work in the world, the work that may not cease, and sat along the gallows branches and chirruped to the soul of Tom, the soul that might not go free. All the thoughts that he had ever uttered! And the evil thoughts rebuked the soul that bore them because they might not die. And all those that he had uttered the most furtively, chirruped the loudest and the shrillest in the branches all the night.

And all the thoughts that Tom had ever thought about himself now pointed at the wet bones and mocked at the old torn coat. But the thoughts that he had had of others were the only companions that his soul had to soothe it in the night as it swung to and fro. And they twittered to the soul and cheered the poor dumb thing that could have dreams no more, till there came a murderous thought and drove them all away.

And the wind blew and blew.

Paul, Archbishop of Alois and Vayence, lay in his white

sepulchre of marble, facing full to the southwards towards
Paradise. And over his tomb was sculptured the Cross of
Christ, that his soul might have repose. No wind howled
here as it howled in lonely tree-tops up upon the downs,
but came with gentle breezes, orchard scented, over the low
lands from Paradise from the southwards, and played about
forget-me-nots and grasses in the consecrated land where lay
the Reposeful round the sepulchre of Paul, Archbishop of
Alois and Vayence. Easy it was for a man's soul to pass
from such a sepulchre, and, flitting low over remembered
fields, to come upon the garden lands of Paradise and find
eternal ease.

And the wind blew and blew.

In a tavern of foul repute three men were lapping gin.
Their names were Joe and Will and the gypsy Puglioni;
no other names had they, for of whom their fathers were
they had no knowledge, but only dark suspicions.

Sin had caressed and stroked their faces often with its
paws, but the face of Puglioni Sin had kissed all over the
mouth and chin. Their food was robbery and their pas-
time murder. All of them had incurred the sorrow of God
and the enmity of man. They sat at a table with a pack
of cards before them, all greasy with the marks of cheating
thumbs. And they whispered to one another over their
gin, but so low that the landlord of the tavern at the other
end of the room could hear only muffled oaths, and knew
not by Whom they swore or what they said.

These three were the staunchest friends that ever God
had given unto a man. And he to whom their friendship
had been given had nothing else besides, saving some bones
that swung in the wind and rain, and an old torn coat and
iron chains, and a soul that might not go free.

But as the night wore on the three friends left their gin
and stole away, and crept down to that graveyard where
rested in his sepulchre Paul, Archbishop of Alois and Vayence. At the edge of the graveyard, but outside the con-

secrated ground, they dug a hasty grave, two digging while one watched in the wind and rain. And the worms that crept in the unhallowed ground wondered and waited.

And the terrible hour of midnight came upon them with its fears, and found them still beside the place of tombs. And the three friends trembled at the horror of such an hour in such a place, and shivered in the wind and drenching rain, but still worked on. And the wind blew and blew.

Soon they had finished. And at once they left the hungry grave with all its worms unfed, and went away over the wet fields stealthily but in haste, leaving the place of tombs behind them in the midnight. And as they went they shivered, and each man as he shivered cursed the rain aloud. And so they came to the spot where they had hidden a ladder and a lantern. There they held long debate whether they should light the lantern, or whether they should go without it for fear of the King's men. But in the end it seemed to them better that they should have the light of the lantern, and risk being taken by the King's men and hanged, than that they should come suddenly face to face in the darkness with whatever one might come face to face with a little after midnight about the Gallows Tree.

On three roads in England whereon it was not the wont of folks to go their ways in safety, travellers to-night went unmolested. But the three friends, walking several paces wide of the King's highway, approached the Gallows Tree, and Will carried the lantern and Joe the ladder, but Puglioni carried a great sword wherewith to do the work which must be done. When they came close, they saw how bad was the case with Tom, for little remained of that fine figure of a man and nothing at all of his great resolute spirit, only as they came they thought they heard a whimpering cry like the sound of a thing that was caged and unfree.

To and fro, to and fro in the winds swung the bones and the soul of Tom, for the sins that he had sinned on the King's highway against the laws of the King; and with shadows and a lantern through the darkness, at the peril of their lives, came the three friends that his soul had won before it swung in chains. Thus the seeds of Tom's own soul that he had sown all his life had grown into a Gallows Tree that bore in season iron chains in clusters; while the careless seeds that he had strewn here and there, a kindly jest and a few merry words, had grown into the triple friendship that would not desert his bones.

Then the three set the ladder against the tree, and Puglioni went up with his sword in his right hand, and at top of it he reached up and began to hack at the neck below the iron collar. Presently, the bones and the old coat and the soul of Tom fell down with a rattle, and a moment afterwards his head that had watched so long alone swung clear from the swinging chain. These things Will and Joe gathered up, and Puglioni came running down his ladder, and they heaped upon its rungs the terrible remains of their friend, and hastened away wet through with the rain, with the fear of phantoms in their hearts and horror lying before them on the ladder. By two o'clock they were down again in the valley out of the bitter wind, but they went on past the open grave into the graveyard all among the tombs, with their lantern and their ladder and the terrible thing upon it, which kept their friendship still. Then these three, that had robbed the Law of its due and proper victim, still sinned on for what was still their friend, and levered out the marble slabs from the sacred sepulchre of Paul, Archbishop of Alois and Vayence. And from it they took the very bones of the Archbishop himself, and carried them away to the eager grave that they had left, and put them in and shovelled back the earth. But all that lay on the ladder they placed, with a few tears, within the great white sepulchre under the Cross of Christ, and put back the marble slabs.

Thence the soul of Tom, arising hallowed out of sacred ground, went at dawn down the valley, and, lingering a little about his mother's cottage and old haunts of childhood, passed

on and came to the wide lands beyond the clustered homesteads. There, there met with it all the kindly thoughts that
the soul of Tom had ever had, and they flew and sang
beside it all the way southwards, until at last, with singing
all about it, it came to Paradise.

But Will and Joe and the gypsy Puglioni went back to
their gin, and robbed and cheated again in the tavern of
foul repute, and knew not that in their sinful lives they had
sinned one sin at which the Angels smiled.

IN THE TWILIGHT

THE lock was quite crowded with boats when we capsized. I went down backwards for some few feet before I started to swim, then I came spluttering upwards towards the light; but, instead of reaching the surface, I hit my head against the keel of a boat and went down again. I struck out almost at once and came up, but before I reached the surface my head crashed against a boat for the second time, and I went right to the bottom. I was confused and thoroughly frightened. I was desperately in need of air, and knew that if I hit a boat for the third time I should never see the surface again. Drowning is a horrible death, notwithstanding all that has been said to the contrary. My past life never occurred to my mind, but I thought of many trivial things that I might not do or see again if I were drowned. I swam up in a slanting direction, hoping to avoid the boat that I had struck. Suddenly I saw all the boats in the lock quite clearly just above me, and every one of their curved varnished planks and the scratches and chips upon their keels. I saw several gaps among the boats where I might have swam up to the surface, but it did not seem worth while to try and get there, and I had forgotten why I wanted to. Then all the people leaned over the sides of their boats: I saw the light flannel suits of the men and the coloured flowers in the women's hats, and I noticed details of their dresses quite distinctly. Everybody in the boats was looking down at me; then they all said to one another,

"We must leave him now," and they and the boats went away; and there was nothing above me but the river and the sky, and on either side of me were the green weeds that grew in the mud, for I had somehow sunk back to the bottom again. The river as it flowed by murmured not unpleasantly in my ears, and the rushes seemed to be whispering quite softly among themselves. Presently the murmuring of the river took the form of words, and I heard it say, "We must go on to the sea; we must leave him now."

Then the river went away, and both its banks; and the rushes whispered, "Yes, we must leave him now." And they too departed, and I was left in a great emptiness staring up at the blue sky. Then the great sky bent over me, and spoke quite softly like a kindly nurse soothing some little foolish child, and the sky said, "Good-bye. All will be well. Goodbye." And I was sorry to lose the blue sky, but the sky went away. Then I was alone, with nothing round about me; I could see no light, but it was not dark—there was just absolutely nothing, above me and below me and on every side. I thought that perhaps I was dead, and that this might be eternity; when suddenly some great southern hills rose up all round about me, and I was lying on the warm, grassy slope of a valley in England. It was a valley that I had known well when I was young, but I had not seen it now for many years. Beside me stood the tall flower of the mint; I saw the sweet-smelling thyme flower and one or two wild strawberries. There came up to me from fields below me the beautiful smell of hay, and there was a break in the voice of the cuckoo. There was a feeling of summer and of evening and of lateness and of Sabbath in the air; the sky was calm and full of a strange colour, and the sun was low; the bells in the church in the village were all a-ring, and the chimes went wandering with echoes up the valley towards the sun, and whenever the echoes died a new chime was born. And all the people of the village walked up a stone-paved path under a black oak porch and went into the church, and the chimes stopped and the people of the village began to sing, and the level sunlight shone on the white tombstones that stood all round the church. Then there was a stillness in the village, and shouts and laughter came up from the valley no more, only the occasional sound of the organ and of song. And the blue butterflies, those that love the chalk, came and perched themselves on the tall grasses, five or six sometimes on a single piece of grass, and they closed their wings and slept, and the grass bent a little beneath them. And from the woods along the tops of the hills the rabbits came hopping out and nibbled the grass, and hopped a little further and nibbled again, and the large daisies closed their petals up and the birds began to sing.

Then the hills spoke, all the great chalk hills that I loved, and with a deep and solemn voice they said, "We have come to you to say Goodbye."

Then they all went away, and there was nothing again all round about me upon every side. I looked everywhere for something on which to rest the eye. Nothing. Suddenly a low grey sky swept over me and a moist air met my face; a great plain rushed up to me from the edge of the clouds; on two sides it touched the sky, and on two sides between it and the clouds a line of low hills lay. One line of hills brooded grey in the distance, the other stood a patchwork of little square green fields, with a few white cottages about it. The plain was an archipelago of a million islands each about a yard square or less, and every one of them was red with heather. I was back on the Bog of Allen again after many years, and it was just the same as ever, though I had heard that they were draining it. I was with an old friend whom I was glad to see again, for they had told me that he died some years ago. He seemed strangely young, but what surprised me most was that he stood upon a piece of bright green moss which I had always learned to think would never bear. I was glad, too, to see the old bog again and all

the lovely things that grew there—the scarlet mosses and
the green mosses and the firm and friendly heather, and the
deep silent water. I saw a little stream that wandered
vaguely through the bog, and little white shells down in the
clear depths of it; I saw, a little way off, one of the great
pools where no islands are, with rushes round its borders,
where the ducks love to come. I looked long at that untroubled world of heather, and then I looked at the white
cottages on the hill, and saw the grey smoke curling from
their chimneys and knew that they burned turf there, and
longed for the smell of burning turf again. And far away
there arose and came nearer the weird cry of wild and happy
voices, and a flock of geese appeared that was coming from
the northward. Then their cries blended into one great
voice of exultation, the voice of freedom, the voice of Ireland, the voice of the Waste; and the voice said "Goodbye
to you. Goodbye!" and passed away into the distance;
and as it passed, the tame geese on the farms cried out to
their brothers up above them that they were free. Then
the hills went away, and the bog and the sky went with
them, and I was alone again, as lost souls are alone.

Then there grew up beside me the red brick buildings of
my first school and the chapel that adjoined it. The fields
a little way off were full of boys in white flannels playing
cricket. On the asphalt playing ground, just by the schoolroom windows, stood Agamemnon, Achilles, and Odysseus,
with their Argives armed behind them; but Hector stepped
down out of a ground-floor window, and in the schoolroom
were all Priam's sons and the Achæans and fair Helen; and
a little farther away the Ten Thousand drifted across the
playground, going up into the heart of Persia to place Cyrus
on his brother's throne. And the boys that I knew called
to me from the fields, and said "Goodbye," and they and
the fields went away; and the Ten Thousand said "Goodbye," each file as they passed me marching swiftly, and
they too disappeared. And Hector and Agamemnon said

"Goodbye," and the host of the Argives and of the Achæans; and they all went away and the old school with them, and I was alone again.

The next scene that filled the emptiness was rather dim: I was being led by my nurse along a little footpath over a common in Surrey. She was quite young. Close by a band of gypsies had lit their fire, near them their romantic caravan stood unhorsed, and the horse cropped grass beside it. It was evening, and the gypsies muttered round their fire in a tongue unknown and strange. Then they all said in English, "Goodbye." And the evening and the common and the camp-fire went away. And instead of this a white highway with darkness and stars below it that led into darkness and stars, but at the near end of the road were common fields and gardens, and there I stood close to a large number of people, men and women. And I saw a man walking alone down the road away from me towards the darkness and the stars, and all the people called him by his name, and the man would not hear them, but walked on down the road, and the people went on calling him by his name. But I became irritated with the man because he would not stop or turn round when so many people called him by his name, and it was a very strange name. And I became weary of hearing the strange name so very often repeated, so that I made a great effort to call him, that he might listen and that the people might stop repeating this strange name. And with the effort I opened my eyes wide, and the name that the people called was my own name, and I lay on the river's bank with men and women bending over me, and my hair was wet.

THE GHOSTS

THE argument that I had with my brother in his great lonely house will scarcely interest my readers. Not those, at least, whom I hope may be attracted by the experiment that I undertook, and by the strange things that befell me in that hazardous region into which so lightly and so ignorantly I allowed my fancy to enter. It was at Oneleigh that I had visited him.

Now Oneleigh stands in a wide isolation, in the midst of a dark gathering of old whispering cedars. They nod their heads together when the North Wind comes, and nod again and agree, and furtively grow still again, and say no more awhile. The North Wind is to them like a nice problem among wise old men; they nod their heads over it, and mutter it all together. They know much, those cedars, they have been there so long. Their grandsires knew Lebanon and the grandsires of these were the servants of the King of Tyre and came to Solomon's court. And amidst these black-haired children of grey-headed Time stood the old house of Oneleigh. I know not how many centuries had lashed against it their evanescent foam of years; but it was still unshattered, and all about it were the things of long ago, as cling strange growths to some sea-defying rock. Here, like the shells of long-dead limpets, was armour that men encased themselves in long ago; here, too, were tapestries of many colours, beautiful as seaweed; no modern flotsam ever drifted hither, no early Victorian furniture, no electric light.

The great trade routes that littered the years with empty meat tins and cheap novels were far from here. Well, well, the centuries will shatter it and drive its fragments on to distant shores. Meanwhile, while it yet stood, I went on a visit there to my brother, and we argued about ghosts. My brother's intelligence on this subject seemed to me to be in need of correction. He mistook things imagined for things having an actual existence; he argued that second-hand evidence of persons having seen ghosts proved ghosts to exist. I said that even if they had seen ghosts, this was no proof at all; nobody believes that there are red rats, though there is plenty of first-hand evidence of men having seen them in delirium. Finally, I said I would see ghosts myself, and continue to argue against their actual existence. So I collected a handful of cigars and drank several cups of very strong tea, and went without my dinner, and retired into a room where there was dark oak and all the chairs were covered with tapestry; and my brother went to bed bored with our argument and trying hard to dissuade me from making myself uncomfortable. All the way up the old stairs as I stood at the bottom of them, and as his candle went winding up and up, I heard him still trying to persuade me to have supper and go to bed.

It was a windy winter, and outside the cedars were muttering I know not what about; but I think that they were Tories of a school long dead, and were troubled about something new. Within, a great damp log upon the fireplace began to squeak and sing, and struck up a whining tune, and a tall flame stood up over it and beat time, and all the shadows crowded round and began to dance. In distant corners old masses of darkness sat still like chaperones and never moved. Over there, in the darkest part of the room, stood a door that was always locked. It led into the hall, but no one ever used it; near that door something had happened once of which the family are not proud. We do not speak of it. There in the firelight stood the venerable form of the old chairs; the hands that had made their tapestries lay far beneath the soil, the needles with which they wrought were many separate flakes of rust. No one wove now in that old room—no one but the assiduous ancient spiders who, watching by the deathbed of the things of yore, worked shrouds to hold their dust. In shrouds about the cornices already lay the heart of the oak wainscot that the worm had eaten out.

Surely at such an hour, in such a room, a fancy already excited by hunger and strong tea might see the ghosts of former occupants. I expected nothing less. The fire flickered and the shadows danced, memories of strange historic things rose vividly in my mind; but midnight chimed solemnly from a seven-foot clock, and nothing happened. My imagination would not be hurried, and the chill that is with the small hours had come upon me, and I had nearly abandoned myself to sleep, when in the hall adjoining there arose the rustling of silk dresses that I had waited for and expected. Then there entered two by two the high-born ladies and their gallants of Jacobean times. They were little more than shadows—very dignified shadows, and almost indistinct; but you have all read ghost stories before, you have all seen in museums the dresses of those times—there is little need to discribe them; they entered, several of them and sat down on the old chairs, perhaps a little carelessly considering the value of the tapestries. Then the rustling of their dresses ceased.

Well—I had seen ghosts, and was neither frightened nor convinced that ghosts existed. I was about to get up out of my chair and go to bed, when there came a sound of pattering in the hall, a sound of bare feet coming over the polished floor, and every now and then a foot would slip and I heard claws scratching along the wood as some four-footed thing lost and regained its balance. I was not frightened, but uneasy. The pattering came straight towards the room that I was in, then I heard the sniffing of expectant nostrils; perhaps "uneasy" was not the most suitable word to describe my feelings then. Suddenly a herd of black creatures larger than bloodhounds came galloping in; they had large pendulous ears, their noses were to the ground sniffing, they went up to the lords and ladies of long ago and fawned about them disgustingly. Their eyes were horribly bright, and ran down to great depths. When I looked into them I knew suddenly what these creatures were, and I was afraid. They were the sins, the filthy, immortal sins of those courtly men and women.

How demure she was, the lady that sat near me on an old-world chair—how demure she was, and how fair, to have beside her with its jowl upon her lap a sin with such cavernous red eyes, a clear case of murder. And you, yonder lady with the golder hair, surely not you—and yet that fearful beast with the yellow eyes slinks from you to yonder courtier there, and whenever one drives it away it slinks back to the other. Over there a lady tries to smile as she strokes the loathsome furry head of another's sin, but one of her own is jealous and intrudes itself under her hand. Here sits an old nobleman with his grandson on his knee, and one of the great black sins of the grandfather is licking the child's face and has made the child its own. Sometimes a ghost would move and seek another chair, but always his pack of sins would move behind him. Poor ghosts, poor ghosts! how many flights they must have attempted for two hundred years from their hated sins, how many excuses they must have given for their presence, and the sins were with them still—and still unexplained. Suddenly one of them seemed to scent my living blood, and bayed horribly, and all the others left their ghosts at once and dashed up to the sin that had given tongue. The brute had picked up my scent near the door by which I had entered, and they moved slowly nearer to me sniffing along the floor, and uttering every now and then their fearful cry. I saw that the whole thing had gone too far. But now they had seen me, now they were all about me, they sprang up trying to reach my throat; and whenever their claws touched me, horrible thoughts came into my mind and unutterable desires dominated my heart. I planned bestial things as these creatures leaped around me, and planned them with a masterly cunning. A great red-eyed murder was among the foremost of those furry things from whom I feebly strove to defend my throat. Suddenly it seemed to me good that I should kill my brother. It seemed important to me that I should not risk being punished. I knew where a revolver was kept; after I had shot him, I would dress the body up and put flour on the face like a man that had been acting as a ghost. It would be very simple. I would say that he had frightened me—and the servants had heard us talking about ghosts. There were one or two trivialities that would have to be arranged, but nothing escaped my mind. Yes, it seemed to me very good that I should kill my brother as I looked into the red depths of this creature's eyes. But one last effort as they dragged me down—"If two straight lines cut one another," I said, "the opposite angles are equal. Let AB, CD, cut one another at E, then the angles CEA, CEB equal two right angles (prop. xiii.). Also CEA, AED equal two right angles."

I moved towards the door to get the revolver; a hideous exultation arose among the beasts. "But the angle CEA is common, therefore AED equals CEB. In the same way CEA equals DEB. Q.E.D." It was proved. Logic and reason re-established themselves in my mind, there were no dark hounds of sin, the tapestried chairs were empty. It seemed to me an inconceivable thought that a man should murder his brother.

THE WHIRLPOOL

ONCE going down to the shore of the great sea I came upon the Whirlpool lying prone upon the sand and stretching his huge limbs in the sun.

I said to him: "Who art thou?"

And he said:

"I am named Nooz Wana, the Whelmer of Ships, and from the Straits of Pondar Obed I am come, wherein it is my wont to vex the seas. There I chased Leviathan with my hands when he was young and strong; often he slipped through my fingers, and away into the weed forests that grow below the storms in the dusk on the floor of the sea; but at last I caught and tamed him. For there I lurk upon the ocean's floor, midway between the knees of either cliff, to guard the passage of the Straits from all the ships that seek the Further Seas; and whenever the white sails of the tall ships come swelling round the corner of the crag out of the sunlit spaces of the Known Sea and into the dark of the Straits, then standing firm upon the ocean's floor, with my knees a little bent, I take the waters of the Straits in both my hands and whirl them round my head. But the ship comes gliding on with the sound of the sailors singing on her decks, all singing songs of the islands and carrying the rumour of their cities to the lonely seas, till they see me suddenly astride athwart their course, and are caught in the waters as I whirl them round my head. Then I draw in the waters of the Straits towards me and downwards, nearer and

175

nearer to my terrible feet, and hear in my ears above the roar of my waters the ultimate cry of the ship; for just before I drag them to the floor of ocean and stamp them asunder with my wrecking feet, ships utter their ultimate cry, and with it go the lives of all the sailors and passes the soul of the ship. And in the ultimate cry of ships are the songs the sailors sing, and their hopes and all their loves, and the song of the wind among the masts and timbers when they stood in the forest long ago, and the whisper of the rain that made them grow, and the soul of the tall pine-tree or the oak. All this a ship gives up in one cry which she makes at the last. And at that moment I would pity the tall ship if I might; but a man may feel pity who sits in comfort by his fireside telling tales in the winter— no pity are they permitted ever to feel who do the work of the gods; and so when I have brought her circling from round my shoulders to my waist and thence, with her masts all sloping inwards, to my knees, and lower still and downwards till her topmast pennants flutter against my ankles, then I, Nooz Wana, Whelmer of Ships, lift up my feet and trample her beams asunder, and there go up again to the surface of the Straits only a few broken timbers and the memories of the sailors and of their early loves to drift for ever down the empty seas.

"Once in every hundred years, for one day only, I go to rest myself along the shore and to sun my limbs on the sand, that the tall ships may go through the unguarded Straits and find the Happy Isles. And the Happy Isles stand midmost among the smiles of the sunny Further Seas, and there the sailors may come upon content and long for nothing; or if they long for aught, they shall possess it.

"There comes not Time with his devouring hours; nor any of the evils of the gods or men. These are the islands whereto the souls of the sailors every night put in from all the world to rest from going up and down the seas, to behold again the vision of far-off intimate hills that lift their orchards high above the fields facing the sunlight, and for a while again to speak with the souls of old. But about the dawn dreams twitter and arise, and circling thrice around the Happy Isles set out again to find the world of men, then follow the souls of the sailors, as, at evening, with slow stroke of stately wings the heron follows behind the flight of multitudinous rooks; but the souls returning find awakening bodies and endure the toil of the day. Such are the Happy Isles, whereunto few have come, save but as roaming shadows in the night, and for only a little while.

"But longer than is needed to make me strong and fierce again I may not stay, and at set of sun, when my arms are strong again and when I feel in my legs that I can plant them fair and bent upon the floor of ocean, then I go back to take a new grip upon the waters of the Straits, and to guard the Further Seas again for a hundred years. Because the gods are jealous, lest too many men shall pass to the Happy Isles and find content. *For the gods have not content.*"

THE HURRICANE

O NE night I sat alone on the great down, looking over the edge of it at a murky, sullen city. All day long with its smoke it had troubled the holy sky, and now it sat there roaring in the distance and glared at me with its furnaces and lighted factory windows. Suddenly I became aware that I was not the only enemy of that city, for I perceived the colossal form of the Hurricane walking over the down towards me, playing idly with the flowers as he passed, and near me he stopped and spake to the Earthquake, who had come up mole-like but vast out of a cleft in the earth.

"Old friend," said the Hurricane, "rememberest when we wrecked the nations and drave the herds of the sea into new pasturage?"

"Yes," said the Earthquake, drowsily; "Yes, yes."

"Old friend," said the Hurricane, "there are cities everywhere. Over thy head while thou didst sleep they have built them constantly. My four children the Winds suffocate with the fumes of them, the valleys are desolate of flowers, and the lovely forests are cut down since last we went abroad together."

The Earthquake lay there, with his snout towards the city blinking at the lights, while the tall Hurricane stood beside him pointing fiercely at it.

"Come," said the Hurricane, "let us fare forth again and destroy them, that all the lovely forests may come back and the furry creeping things. Thou shalt whelm these cities

178

utterly and drive the people forth, and I will smite them in the shelterless places and sweep their desecrations from the sea. Wilt thou come forth with me and do this thing for the glory of it? Wilt thou wreck the world again as we did, thou and I, or ever Man had come? Wilt thou come forth to this place at this hour to-morrow night?"

"Yes," said the Earthquake, "Yes," and he crept to his cleft again, and head foremost waddled down into the abysses.

When the Hurricane strode away, I got up quietly and departed, but at that hour of the next night I came up cautiously to the same spot. There I found the huge grey form of the Hurricane alone, with his head bowed in his hands, weeping; for the Earthquake sleeps long and heavily in the abysses, and he would not wake.

THE FORTRESS UNVANQUISHABLE
SAVE FOR SACNOTH

IN a wood older than record, a foster brother of the hills, stood the village of Allathurion; and there was peace between the people of that village and all the folk who walked in the dark ways of the wood, whether they were human or of the tribes of the beasts or of the race of the fairies and the elves and the little sacred spirits of trees and streams. Moreover, the village people had peace among themselves and between them and their lord, Lorendiac. In front of the village was a wide and grassy space, and beyond this the great wood again, but at the back the trees came right up to the houses, which, with their great beams and wooden framework and thatched roofs, green with moss, seemed almost to be a part of the forest.

Now in the time I tell of, there was trouble in Allathurion, for of an evening fell dreams were wont to come slipping through the tree trunks and into the peaceful village; and they assumed dominion of men's minds and led them in watches of the night through the cindery plains of Hell. Then the magician of that village made spells against those fell dreams; yet still the dreams came flitting through the trees as soon as the dark had fallen, and led men's minds by night into terrible places and caused them to praise Satan openly with their lips.

And men grew afraid of sleep in Allathurion. And they grew worn and pale, some through the want of rest, and others from fear of the things they saw on the cindery plains of Hell.

Then the magician of the village went up into the tower of his house, and all night long those whom fear kept awake could see his window high up in the night glowing softly alone. The next day, when the twilight was far gone and night was gathering fast, the magician went away to the forest's edge, and uttered there the spell that he had made. And the spell was a compulsive, terrible thing, having a power over evil dreams and over spirits of ill; for it was a verse of forty lines in many languages, both living and dead, and had in it the word wherewith the people of the plains are wont to curse their camels, and the shout wherewith the whalers of the north lure the whales shoreward to be killed, and a word that causes elephants to trumpet; and every one of the forty lines closed with a rhyme for "wasp."

And still the dreams came flitting through the forest, and led men's souls into the plains of Hell. Then the magician knew that the dreams were from Gaznak. Therefore he gathered the people of the village, and told them that he had uttered his mightiest spell—a spell having power over all that were human or of the tribes of the beasts; and that since it had not availed the dreams must come from Gaznak, the greatest magician among the spaces of the stars. And he read to the people out of the Book of Magicians, which tells the comings of the comet and foretells his coming again. And he told them how Gaznak rides upon the comet, and how he visits Earth once in every two hundred and thirty years, and makes for himself a vast, invincible fortress and sends out dreams to feed on the minds of men, and may never be vanquished but by the sword Sacnoth.

And a cold fear fell on the hearts of the villagers when they found that their magician had failed them.

Then spake Leothric, son of the Lord Lorendiac, and twenty years old was he: "Good Master, what of the sword Sacnoth?"

And the village magician answered: "Fair Lord, no such sword as yet is wrought, for it lies as yet in the hide of Tharagavverug, protecting his spine."

Then said Leothric: "Who is Tharagavverug, and where may he be encountered?"

And the magician of Allathurion answered: "He is the dragon-crocodile who haunts the Northern marshes and ravages the homesteads by their marge. And the hide of his back is of steel, and his under parts are of iron; but along the midst of his back, over his spine, there lies a narrow strip of unearthly steel. This strip of steel is Sacnoth, and it may be neither cleft nor molten, and there is nothing in the world that may avail to break it, nor even leave a scratch upon its surface. It is of the length of a good sword, and of the breadth thereof. Shouldst thou prevail against Tharagavverug, his hide may be melted away from Sacnoth in a furnace; but there is only one thing that may sharpen Sacnoth's edge, and this is one of Tharagavverug's own steel eyes; and the other eye thou must fasten to Sacnoth's hilt, and it will watch for thee. But it is a hard task to vanquish Tharagavverug, for no sword can pierce his hide; his back cannot be broken, and he can neither burn nor drown. In one way only can Tharagavverug die, and that is by starving."

Then sorrow fell upon Leothric, but the magician spoke on:

"If a man drive Tharagavverug away from his food with a stick for three days, he will starve on the third day at sunset. And though he is not vulnerable, yet in one spot he may take hurt, for his nose is only of lead. A sword would merely lay bare the uncleavable bronze beneath, but if his nose be smitten constantly with a stick he will always recoil from the pain, and thus may Tharagavverug, to left and right, be driven away from his food."

Then Leothric said: "What is Tharagavverug's food?"

And the magician of Allathurion said: "His food is men."

But Leothric went straightway thence, and cut a great staff from a hazel tree, and slept early that evening. But the next morning, awaking from troubled dreams, he arose before the dawn, and, taking with him provisions for five days, set out through the forest northwards towards the marshes. For some hours he moved through the gloom of the forest, and when he emerged from it the sun was above the horizon shining on pools of water in the waste land. Presently he saw the claw-marks of Tharagavverug deep in the soil, and the track of his tail between them like a furrow in a field. Then Leothric followed the tracks till he heard the bronze heart of Tharagavverug before him, booming like a bell.

And Tharagavverug, it being the hour when he took the first meal of the day, was moving toward a village with his heart tolling. And all the people of the village were come out to meet him, as it was their wont to do; for they abode not the suspense of awaiting Tharagavverug and of hearing him sniffing brazenly as he went from door to door, pondering slowly in his metal mind what habitant he should choose. And none dared to flee, for in the days when the villagers fled from Tharagavverug, he, having chosen his victim, would track him tirelessly, like a doom. Nothing availed them against Tharagavverug. Once they climbed the trees when he came, but Tharagavverug went up to one, arching his back and leaning over slightly, and rasped against the trunk until it fell. And when Leothric came near, Tharagavverug saw him out of one of his small steel eyes and came towards him leisurely, and the echoes of his heart swirled up through his open mouth. And Leothric stepped sideways from his onset, and came between him and the village and smote him on the nose, and the blow of the stick made a dint in the soft lead. And Tharagavverug swung clumsily away, uttering one fearful cry like the sound of a great church bell that had become possessed of a soul that fluttered upward from the tombs at night—an evil soul, giving the bell a voice.

Then he attacked Leothric, snarling, and again Leothric leapt aside, and smote him on the nose with his stick. Tharagavverug uttered like a bell howling. And whenever the dragon-crocodile attacked him, or turned towards the village, Leothric smote him again.

So all day long Leothric drove the monster with a stick and he drove him farther and farther from his prey, with his heart tolling angrily and his voice crying out for pain.

Towards evening Tharagavverug ceased to snap at Leothric, but ran before him to avoid the stick, for his nose was sore and shining; and in the gloaming the villagers came out and danced to cymbal and psaltery. When Tharagavverug heard the cymbal and psaltery, hunger and anger came upon him, and he felt as some lord might feel who was held by force from the banquet in his own castle and heard the creaking spit go round and round and the good meat crackling on it. And all that night he attacked Leothric fiercely, and oft-times nearly caught him in the darkness; for his gleaming eyes of steel could see as well by night as by day. And Leothric gave ground slowly till the dawn, and when the light came they were near the village again; yet not so near to it as they had been when they encountered, for Leothric drove Tharagavverug farther in the day than Tharagavverug had forced him back in the night. Then Leothric drove him again with his stick till the hour came when it was the custom of the dragon-crocodile to find his man. One third of his man he would eat at the time he found him, and the rest at noon and evening. But when the hour came for finding his man a great fierceness came on Tharagavverug, and he grabbed rapidly at Leothric, but could not seize him, and for a long while neither of them would retire. But at last the pain of the stick on his leaden nose overcame the hunger of the dragon-crocodile, and he turned from it howling. From that moment Tharagavverug weakened. All that day Leothric drove him with his stick, and at night both held their ground; and when the dawn of the third day was

come the heart of Tharagavverug beat slower and fainter.
It was as though a tired man was ringing a bell. Once
Tharagavverug nearly seized a frog, but Leothric snatched
it away just in time. Towards noon the dragon-crocodile
lay still for a long while, and Leothric stood near him and
leaned on his trusty stick. He was very tired and sleepless,
but had more leisure now for eating his provisions. With
Tharagavverug the end was coming fast, and in the afternoon his breath came hoarsely, rasping in his throat. It was
as the sound of many huntsmen blowing blasts on horns,
and towards evening his breath came faster but fainter, like
the sound of a hunt going furious to the distance and dying
away, and he made desperate rushes towards the village;
but Leothric still leapt about him, battering his leaden nose.
Scarce audible now at all was the sound of his heart: it was
like a church bell tolling beyond hills for the death of some
one unknown and far away. Then the sun set and flamed
in the village windows, and a chill went over the world, and
in some small garden a woman sang; and Tharagavverug
lifted up his head and starved, and his life went from his
invulnerable body, and Leothric lay down beside him and
slept. And later in the starlight the villagers came out and
carried Leothric, sleeping, to the village, all praising him in
whispers as they went. They laid him down upon a couch
in a house, and danced outside in silence, without psaltery
or cymbal. And the next day, rejoicing, to Allathurion they
hauled the dragon-crocodile. And Leothric went with them,
holding his battered staff; and a tall, broad man, who was
smith of Allthurion, made a great furnace, and melted Tharagavverug away till only Sacnoth was left, gleaming among
the ashes. Then he took one of the small eyes that had been
chiselled out, and filed an edge on Sacnoth, and gradually
the steel eye wore away facet by facet, but ere it was quite
gone it had sharpened redoubtably Sacnoth. But the other
eye they set in the butt of the hilt, and it gleamed there
bluely.

And that night Leothric arose in the dark and took the sword, and went westwards to find Gaznak; and he went through the dark forest till the dawn, and all the morning and till the afternoon. But in the afternoon he came into the open and saw in the midst of The Land Where No Man Goeth the fortress of Gaznak, mountainous before him, little more than a mile away.

And Leothric saw that the land was marsh and desolate. And the fortress went up all white out of it, with many buttresses, and was broad below but narrowed higher up, and was full of gleaming windows with the light upon them. And near the top of it a few white clouds were floating, but above them some of its pinnacles reappeared. Then Leothric advanced into the marshes, and the eye of Tharagavverug looked out warily from the hilt of Sacnoth; for Tharagavverug had known the marshes well, and the sword nudged Leothric to the right or pulled him to the left away from the dangerous places, and so brought him safely to the fortress walls.

And in the wall stood doors like precipices of steel, all studded with boulders of iron, and above every window were terrible gargoyles of stone; and the name of the fortress shone on the wall, writ large in letters of brass: "The Fortress Unvanquishable, Save For Sacnoth."

Then Leothric drew and revealed Sacnoth, and all the gargoyles grinned, and the grin went flickering from face to face right up into the cloud-abiding gables.

And when Sacnoth was revealed and all the gargoyles grinned, it was like the moonlight emerging from a cloud to look for the first time upon a field of blood, and passing swiftly over the wet faces of the slain that lie together in the horrible night. Then Leothric advanced towards a door, and it was mightier than the marble quarry, Sacremona, from which of old men cut enormous slabs to build the Abbey of the Holy Tears. Day after day they wrenched out the very ribs of the hill until the Abbey was builded, and it was more beautiful than anything in stone. Then the priests blessed Sacremona, and it had rest, and no more stone was ever taken from it to build the houses of men. And the hill stood looking southwards lonely in the sunlight, defaced by that mighty scar. So vast was the door of steel. And the name of the door was The Porte Resonant, the Way of Egress for War.

Then Leothric smote upon the Porte Resonant with Sacnoth, and the echo of Sacnoth went ringing through the halls, and all the dragons in the fortress barked. And when the baying of the remotest dragon had faintly joined in the tumult, a window opened far up among the clouds below the twilit gables, and a woman screamed, and far away in Hell her father heard her and knew that her doom was come.

And Leothric went on smiting terribly with Sacnoth, and the grey steel of the Porte Resonant, the Way of Egress for War, that was tempered to resist the swords of the world, came away in ringing slices.

Then Leothric, holding Sacnoth in his hand, went in through the hole that he had hewn in the door, and came into the unlit, cavernous hall.

An elephant fled trumpeting. And Leothric stood still, holding Sacnoth. When the sound of the feet of the elephant had died away in remoter corridors, nothing more stirred, and the cavernous hall was still.

Presently the darkness of the distant halls became musical with the sound of bells, all coming nearer and nearer.

Still Leothric waited in the dark, and the bells rang louder and louder, echoing through the halls, and there appeared a procession of men on camels riding two by two from the interior of the fortress, and they were armed with scimitars of Assyrian make and were all clad with mail, and chainmail hung from their helmets about their faces, and flapped as the camels moved. And they all halted before Leothric in the cavernous hall, and the camel bells clanged and stopped. And the leader said to Leothric:

"The Lord Gaznak has desired to see you die before him.

Be pleased to come with us, and we can discourse by the way of the manner in which the Lord Gaznak has desired to see you die."

And as he said this he unwound a chain of iron that was coiled upon his saddle, and Leothric answered:

"I would fain go with you, for I am come to slay Gaznak."

Then all the camel-guard of Gaznak laughed hideously, disturbing the vampires that were asleep in the measureless vault of the roof. And the leader said:

"The Lord Gaznak is immortal, save for Sacnoth, and weareth armour that is proof even against Sacnoth himself, and hath a sword the second most terrible in the world."

Then Leothric said: "I am the Lord of the sword Sacnoth."

And he advanced towards the camel-guard of Gaznak, and Sacnoth lifted up and down in his hand as though stirred by an exultant pulse. Then the camel-guard of Gaznak fled, and the riders leaned forward and smote their camels with whips, and they went away with a great clamour of bells through colonnades and corridors and vaulted halls, and scattered into the inner darknesses of the fortress. When the last sound of them had died away, Leothric was in doubt which way to go, for the camel-guard was dispersed in many directions, so he went straight on till he came to a great stairway in the midst of the hall. Then Leothric set his foot in the middle of a wide step, and climbed steadily up the stairway for five minutes. Little light was there in the great hall through which Leothric ascended, for it only entered through arrow slits here and there, and in the world outside evening was waning fast. The stairway led up to two folding doors, and they stood a little ajar, and through the crack Leothric entered and tried to continue straight on, but could get no farther, for the whole room seemed to be full of festoons of ropes which swung from wall to wall and were looped and draped from the ceiling. The whole chamber was thick and black with them. They were soft and

light to the touch, like fine silk, but Leothric was unable to
break any one of them, and though they swung away from
him as he pressed forward, yet by the time he had gone
three yards they were all about him like a heavy cloak. Then
Leothric stepped back and drew Sacnoth, and Sacnoth divided
the ropes without a sound, and without a sound the severed
pieces fell to the floor. Leothric went forward slowly, moving Sacnoth in front of him up and down as he went. When
he was come into the middle of the chamber, suddenly, as
he parted with Sacnoth a great hammock of strands, he saw
a spider before him that was larger than a ram, and the
spider looked at him with eyes that were little, but in which
there was much sin, and said:

"Who are you that spoil the labour of years all done to
the honour of Satan?"

And Leothric answered: "I am Leothric, son of Lorendiac."

And the spider said: "I will make a rope at once to hang
you with."

Then Leothric parted another bunch of strands, and came
nearer to the spider as he sat making his rope, and the
spider, looking up from his work, said: "What is that
sword which is able to sever my ropes?"

And Leothric said: "It is Sacnoth."

Thereat the black hair that hung over the face of the
spider parted to left and right, and the spider frowned:
then the hair fell back into its place, and hid everything
except the sin of the little eyes which went on gleaming
lustfully in the dark. But before Leothric could reach him,
he climbed away with his hands, going up by one of his
ropes to a lofty rafter, and there sat, growling. But clearing
his way with Sacnoth, Leothric passed through the chamber,
and came to the farther door; and the door being shut, and
the handle far up out of his reach, he hewed his way through
it with Sacnoth in the same way as he had through the
Porte Resonant, the Way of Egress for War. And so

Leothric came into a well-lit chamber, where Queens and Princes were banqueting together, all at a great table; and thousands of candles were glowing all about, and their light shone in the wine that the Princes drank and on the huge gold candelabra, and the royal faces were irradiant with the glow, and the white table-cloth and the silver plates and the jewels in the hair of the Queens, each jewel having a historian all to itself, who wrote no other chronicles all his days. Between the table and the door there stood two hundred footmen in two rows of one hundred facing one another. Nobody looked at Leothric as he entered through the hole in the door, but one of the Princes asked a question of a footman, and the question was passed from mouth to mouth by all the hundred footmen till it came to the last one nearest Leothric; and he said to Leothric, without looking at him:

"What do you seek here?"

And Leothric answered: "I seek to slay Gaznak."

And footman to footman repeated all the way to the table: "He seeks to slay Gaznak."

And another question came down the line of footmen: "What is your name?"

And the line that stood opposite took his answer back.

Then one of the Princes said: "Take him away where we shall not hear his screams."

And footman repeated it to footman till it came to the last two, and they advanced to seize Leothric.

Then Leothric showed to them his sword, saying, "This is Sacnoth," and both of them said to the man nearest: "It is Sacnoth;" then screamed and fled away.

And two by two, all up the double line, footman to footman repeated, "It is Sacnoth," then screamed and fled, till the last two gave the message to the table, and all the rest had gone. Hurriedly then arose the Queens and Princes, and fled out of the chamber. And the goodly table, when they were all gone, looked small and disorderly and awry.

And to Leothric, pondering in the desolate chamber by what door he should pass onwards, there came from far away the sounds of music, and he knew that it was the magical musicians playing to Gaznak while he slept.

Then Leothric, walking towards the distant music, passed out by the door opposite to the one through which he had cloven his entrance, and so passed into a chamber vast as the other, in which were many women, weirdly beautiful. And they all asked him of his quest, and when they heard that it was to slay Gaznak, they all besought him to tarry among them, saying that Gaznak was immortal, save for Sacnoth, and also that they had need of a knight to protect them from the wolves that rushed round and round the wainscot all the night and sometimes broke in upon them through the mouldering oak. Perhaps Leothric had been tempted to tarry had they been human women, for theirs was a strange beauty, but he perceived that instead of eyes they had little flames that flickered in their sockets, and knew them to be the fevered dreams of Gaznak. Therefore he said:

"I have a business with Gaznak and with Sacnoth," and passed on through the chamber.

And at the name of Sacnoth those women screamed, and the flames of their eyes sank low and dwindled to sparks.

And Leothric left them, and, hewing with Sacnoth, passed through the farther door.

Outside he felt the night air on his face, and found that he stood upon a narrow way between two abysses. To left and right of him, as far as he could see, the walls of the fortress ended in a profound precipice, though the roof still stretched above him; and before him lay the two abysses full of stars, for they cut their way through the whole Earth and revealed the under sky; and threading its course between them went the way, and it sloped upward and its sides were sheer. And beyond the abysses, where the way led up to the farther chambers of the fortress, Leothric heard the musicians playing their magical tune. So he stepped on to the way, which was scarcely a stride in width, and moved along it holding Sacnoth naked. And to and fro beneath him in each abyss whirred the wings of vampires passing up and down, all giving praise to Satan as they flew. Presently he perceived the dragon Thok lying upon the way, pretending to sleep, and his tail hung down into one of the abysses.

And Leothric went towards him, and when he was quite close Thok rushed at Leothric.

And he smote deep with Sacnoth, and Thok tumbled into the abyss, screaming, and his limbs made a whirring in the darkness as he fell, and he fell till his scream sounded no louder than a whistle and then could be heard no more. Once or twice Leothric saw a star blink for an instant and reappear again, and this momentary eclipse of a few stars was all that remained in the world of the body of Thok. And Lunk, the brother of Thok, who had lain a little behind him, saw that this must be Sacnoth and fled lumbering away. And all the while that he walked between the abysses, the mighty vault of the roof of the fortress still stretched over Leothric's head, all filled with gloom. Now, when the farther side of the abyss came into view, Leothric saw a chamber that opened with innumerable arches upon the twin abysses, and the pillars of the arches went away into the distance and vanished in the gloom to left and right.

Far down the dim precipice on which the pillars stood he could see windows small and closely barred, and between the bars there showed at moments, and disappeared again, things that I shall not speak of.

There was no light here except for the great Southern stars that shone below the abysses, and here and there in the chamber through the arches lights that moved furtively without the sound of footfall.

Then Leothric stepped from the way, and entered the great chamber.

Even to himself he seemed but a tiny dwarf as he walked under one of those colossal arches.

The last faint light of evening flickered through a window painted in sombre colours commemorating the achievements of Satan upon Earth. High up in the wall the window stood, and the streaming lights of candles lower down moved stealthily away.

Other light there was none, save for a faint blue glow from the steel eye of Tharagavverug that peered restlessly about it from the hilt of Sacnoth. Heavily in the chamber hung the clammy odour of a large and deadly beast.

Leothric moved forward slowly with the blade of Sacnoth in front of him feeling for a foe, and the eye in the hilt of it looking out behind.

Nothing stirred.

If anything lurked behind the pillars of the colonnade that held aloft the roof, it neither breathed nor moved.

The music of the magical musicians sounded from very near.

Suddenly the great doors on the far side of the chamber opened to left and right. For some moments Leothric saw nothing move, and waited clutching Sacnoth. Then Wong Bongerok came towards him, breathing.

This was the last and faithfullest guard of Gaznak, and came from slobbering just now his master's hand.

More as a child than a dragon was Gaznak wont to treat him, giving him often in his fingers tender pieces of man all smoking from his table.

Long and low was Wong Bongerok, and subtle about the eyes, and he came breathing malice against Leothric out of his faithful breast, and behind him roared the armoury of his tail, as when sailors drag the cable of the anchor all rattling down the deck.

And well Wong Bongerok knew that he now faced Sacnoth, for it had been his wont to prophesy quietly to himself for many years as he lay curled at the feet of Gaznak.

And Leothric stepped forward into the blast of his breath, and lifted Sacnoth to strike.

But when Sacnoth was lifted up, the eye of Tharagavverug in the butt of the hilt beheld the dragon and perceived his subtlety.

For he opened his mouth wide, and revealed to Leothric the ranks of his sabre teeth, and his leather gums flapped upwards. But while Leothric made to smite at his head, he shot forward scorpion-wise over his head the length of his armoured tail. All this the eye perceived in the hilt of Sacnoth, who smote suddenly sideways. Not with the edge smote Sacnoth, for, had he done so, the severed end of the tail had still come hurtling on, as some pine tree that the avalanche has hurled point foremost from the cliff right through the broad breast of some mountaineer. So had Leothric been transfixed; but Sacnoth smote sideways with the flat of his blade, and sent the tail whizzing over Leothric's left shoulder; and it rasped upon his armour as it went, and left a groove upon it. Sideways then at Leothric smote the foiled tail of Wong Bongerok, and Sacnoth parried, and the tail went shrieking up the blade and over Leothric's head. Then Leothric and Wong Bongerok fought sword to tooth, and the sword smote as only Sacnoth can, and the evil faithful life of Wong Bongerok the dragon went out through the wide wound.

Then Leothric walked on past that dead monster, and the armoured body still quivered a little. And for a while it was like all the ploughshares in a county working together in one field behind tired and struggling horses; then the quivering ceased, and Wong Bongerok lay still to rust.

And Leothric went on to the open gates, and Sacnoth dripped quietly along the floor.

By the open gates through which Wong Bongerok had entered, Leothric came into a corridor echoing with music. This was the first place from which Leothric could see anything above his head, for hitherto the roof had ascended to

mountainous heights and had stretched indistinct in the
gloom. But along the narrow corridor hung huge bells low
and near to his head, and the width of each brazen bell was
from wall to wall, and they were one behind the other. And
as he passed under each the bell uttered, and its voice was
mournful and deep, like to the voice of a bell speaking to
a man or the last time when he is newly dead. Each bell
uttered once as Leothric came under it, and their voices
sounded solemnly and wide apart at ceremonious intervals.
For if he walked slow, these bells came closer together, and
when he walked swiftly they moved farther apart. And
the echoes of each bell tolling above his head went on before
him whispering to the others. Once when he stopped they
all jangled angrily till he went on again.

Between these slow and boding notes came the sound of
the magical musicians. They were playing a dirge now very
mournfully.

And at last Leothric came to the end of the Corridor of
the Bells, and beheld there a small black door. And all the
corridor behind him was full of the echoes of the tolling, and
they all muttered to one another about the ceremony; and
the dirge of the musicians came floating slowly through them
like a procession of foreign elaborate guests, and all of them
boded ill to Leothric.

The black door opened at once to the hand of Leothric,
and he found himself in the open air in a wide court paved
with marble. High over it shone the moon, summoned there
by the hand of Gaznak.

There Gaznak slept, and around him sat his magical musicians, all playing upon strings. And, even sleeping, Gaznak
was clad in armour, and only his wrists and face and neck
were bare.

But the marvel of that place was the dreams of Gaznak;
for beyond the wide court slept a dark abyss, and into the
abyss there poured a white cascade of marble stairways, and
widened out below into terraces and balconies with fair white

statues on them, and descended again in a wide stairway, and came to lower terraces in the dark, where swart uncertain shapes went to and fro. All these were the dreams of Gaznak, and issued from his mind, and, becoming marble, passed over the edge of the abyss as the musicians played. And all the while out of the mind of Gaznak, lulled by that strange music, went spires and pinnacles beautiful and slender, ever ascending skywards. And the marble dreams moved slow in time to the music. When the bells tolled and the musicians played their dirge, ugly gargoyles came out suddenly all over the spires and pinnacles, and great shadows passed swiftly down the steps and terraces, and there was hurried whispering in the abyss.

When Leothric stepped from the black door, Gaznak opened his eyes. He looked neither to left nor right, but stood up at once facing Leothric.

Then the magicians played a deathspell on their strings, and there arose a humming along the blade of Sacnoth as he turned the spell aside. When Leothric dropped not down, and they heard the humming of Sacnoth, the magicians arose and fled, all wailing, as they went, upon their strings.

Then Gaznak drew out screaming from its sheath the sword that was the mightiest in the world except for Sacnoth, and slowly walked towards Leothric; and he smiled as he walked, although his own dreams had foretold his doom. And when Leothric and Gaznak came together, each looked at each, and neither spoke a word; but they smote both at once, and their swords met, and each sword knew the other and from whence he came. And whenever the sword of Gaznak smote on the blade of Sacnoth it rebounded gleaming, as hail from off slated roofs; but whenever it fell upon the armour of Leothric, it stripped it off in sheets. And upon Gaznak's armour Sacnoth fell oft and furiously, but ever he came back snarling, leaving no mark behind, and as Gaznak fought he held his left hand hovering close over his head. Presently Leothric smote fair and fiercely at his enemy's neck, but

Gaznak, clutching his own head by the hair, lifted it high aloft, and Sacnoth went cleaving through an empty space. Then Gaznak replaced his head upon his neck, and all the while fought nimbly with his sword; and again and again Leothric swept with Sacnoth at Gaznak's bearded neck, and ever the left hand of Gaznak was quicker than the stroke, and the head went up and the sword rushed vainly under it.

And the ringing fight went on till Leothric's armour lay all round him on the floor and the marble was splashed with his blood, and the sword of Gaznak was notched like a saw from meeting the blade of Sacnoth. Still Gaznak stood unwounded and smiling still.

At last Leothric looked at the throat of Gaznak and aimed with Sacnoth, and again Gaznak lifted his head by the hair; but not at his throat flew Sacnoth, for Leothric struck instead at the lifted hand, and through the wrist of it went Sacnoth whirring, as a scythe goes through the stem of a single flower.

And bleeding, the severed hand fell to the floor; and at once blood spurted from the shoulders of Gaznak and dripped from the fallen head, and the tall pinnacles went down into the earth, and the wide fair terraces all rolled away, and the court was gone like the dew, and a wind came and the colonnades drifted thence, and all the colossal halls of Gaznak fell. And the abysses closed up suddenly as the mouth of a man who, having told a tale, will for ever speak no more.

Then Leothric looked around him in the marshes where the night mist was passing away, and there was no fortress nor sound of dragon or mortal, only beside him lay an old man, wizened and evil and dead, whose head and hand were severed from his body.

And gradually over the wide lands the dawn was coming up, and ever growing in beauty as it came, like to the peal of an organ played by a master's hand, growing louder and lovelier as the soul of the master warms, and at last giving praise with all its mighty voice.

Then the birds sang, and Leothric went homeward, and left the marshes and came to the dark wood, and the light of the dawn ascending lit him upon his way. And into Allathurion he came ere noon, and with him brought the evil wizened head, and the people rejoiced, and their nights of trouble ceased.

*   *   *   *   *   *   *

This is the tale of the vanquishing of The Fortress Unvanquishable, Save For Sacnoth, and of its passing away, as it is told and believed by those who love the mystic days of old.

Others have said, and vainly claim to prove, that a fever came to Allathurion, and went away; and that this same fever drove Leothric into the marshes by night, and made him dream there and act violently with a sword.

And others again say that there hath been no town of Allathurion, and that Leothric never lived.

Peace to them. The gardener hath gathered up this autumn's leaves. Who shall see them again, or who wot of them? And who shall say what hath befallen in the days of long ago?

THE LORD OF CITIES

I CAME one day upon a road that wandered so aimlessly that it was suited to my mood, so I followed it, and it led me presently among deep woods. Somewhere in the midst of them Autumn held his court, sitting wreathed with gorgeous garlands; and it was the day before his annual festival of the Dance of Leaves, the courtly festival upon which hungry Winter rushes mob-like, and there arise the furious cries of the North Wind triumphing, and all the splendour and grace of the woods is gone, and Autumn flees away, discrowned and forgotten, and never again returns. Other Autumns arise, other Autumns, and fall before other Winters. A road led away to the left, but my road went straight on. The road to the left had a trodden appearance; there were wheel tracks on it, and it seemed the correct way to take. It looked as if no one could have any business with the road that led straight on and up the hill. Therefore I went straight on and up the hill; and here and there on the road grew blades of grass undisturbed in the repose and hush that the road had earned from going up and down the world; for you can go by this road, as you can go by all roads, to London, to Lincoln, to the North of Scotland, to the West of Wales, and to Wrellisford where roads end. Presently the woods ended, and I came to the open fields and at the same moment to the top of the hill, and saw the high places of Somerset and the downs of Wilts spread out along the horizon. Suddenly I saw underneath

me the village of Wrellisford, with no sound in its street but
the voice of the Wrellis roaring as he tumbled over a weir
above the village. So I followed my road down over the
crest of the hill, and the road became more languid as I
descended, and less and less concerned with the cares of a
highway. Here a spring broke out in the middle of it, and
here another. The road never heeded. A stream ran right
across it, still it straggled on. Suddenly it gave up the
minimum property that a road should possess, and, renounc-
ing its connection with High Streets, its lineage of Piccadilly,
shrank to one side and became an unpretentious footpath.
Then it led me to the old bridge over the stream, and thus
I came to Wrellisford, and found after travelling in many
lands a village with no wheel tracks in its street. On the
other side of the bridge, my friend the road struggled a few
yards up a grassy slope, and there ceased. Over all the
village hung a great stillness, with the roar of the Wrellis
cutting right across it, and there came occasionally the bark
of a dog that kept watch over the broken stillness and over
the sanctity of that untravelled road. That terrible and
wasting fever that, unlike so many plagues, comes not from
the East but from the West, the fever of hurry, had not come
here—only the Wrellis hurried on his eternal quest, but it
was a calm and placid hurry that gave one time for song.
It was in the early afternoon, and nobody was about. Either
they worked beyond the mysterious valley that nursed Wrellisford and hid it from the world, or else they secluded themselves within their old-time houses that were roofed with
tiles of stone. I sat down upon the old stone bridge and
watched the Wrellis, who seemed to me to be the only
traveller that came from far away into this village where
roads end, and passed on beyond it. And yet the Wrellis
comes singing out of eternity, and tarries for a very little
while in the village where roads end, and passes on into
eternity again; and so surely do all that dwell in Wrellisford.
I wondered as I leaned upon the bridge in what place the

Wrellis would first find the sea, whether as he wound idly through meadows on his long quest he would suddenly behold him, and, leaping down over some rocky cliff, take to him at once the message of the hills. Or whether, widening slowly into some grand and tidal estuary, he would take his waste of waters to the sea and the might of the river should meet with the might of the waves, like to two Emperors clad in gleaming mail meeting midway between two hosts of war; and the little Wrellis would become a haven for returning ships and a setting-out place for adventurous men.

A little beyond the bridge there stood an old mill with a ruined roof, and a small branch of the Wrellis rushed through its emptiness shouting, like a boy playing alone in a corridor of some desolate house. The mill-wheel was gone, but there lay there still great bars and wheels and cogs, the bones of some dead industry. I know not what industry was once lord in that house, I know not what retinue of workers mourns him now; I only know who is lord there to-day in all those empty chambers. For as soon as I entered, I saw a whole wall draped with his marvellous black tapestry, without price because inimitable and too delicate to pass from hand to hand among merchants. I looked at the wonderful complexity of its infinite threads, my finger sank into it for more than an inch without feeling the touch; so black it was and so carefully wrought, sombrely covering the whole of the wall, that it might have been worked to commemorate the deaths of all that ever lived there, as indeed it was. I looked through a hole in the wall into an inner chamber where a worn-out driving band went among many wheels, and there this priceless inimitable stuff not merely clothed the walls but hung from bars and ceiling in beautiful draperies, in marvellous festoons. Nothing was ugly in this desolate house, for the busy artist's soul of its present lord had beautified everything in its desolation. It was the unmistakable work of the spider, in whose house I was, and the house was utterly desolate but for him, and silent but for the roar of the Wrellis and the shout of the little stream. Then I turned homewards; and as I went up and over the hill and lost the sight of the village, I saw the road whiten and harden and gradually broaden out till the tracks of wheels appeared; and it went afar to take the young men of Wrellisford into the wide ways of the earth— to the new West and the mysterious East, and into the troubled South.

And that night, when the house was still and sleep was far off, hushing hamlets and giving ease to cities, my fancy wandered up that aimless road and came suddenly to Wrellisford. And it seemed to me that the travelling of so many people for so many years between Wrellisford and John o' Groat's, talking to one another as they went or muttering alone, had given the road a voice. And it seemed to me that night that the road spoke to the river by Wrellisford bridge, speaking with the voice of many pilgrims. And the road said to the river: "I rest here. How is it with you?"

And the river, who is always speaking, said: "I rest nowhere from doing the Work of the World. I carry the murmur of inner lands to the sea, and to the abysses voices of the hills."

"It is I," said the road, "that do the Work of the World, and take from city to city the rumour of each. There is nothing higher than Man and the making of cities. What do you do for Man?"

And the river said: "Beauty and song are higher than Man. I carry the news seaward of the first song of the thrush after the furious retreat of winter northward, and the first timid anemone learns from me that she is safe and that spring has truly come. Oh but the song of all the birds in spring is more beautiful than Man, and the first coming of the hyacinth more delectable than his face! When spring is fallen upon the days of summer, I carry away with mournful joy at night petal by petal the rhododendron's bloom.

No lit procession of purple kings is nigh so fair as that. No beautiful death of well-beloved men hath such a glory of forlornness. And I bear far away the pink and white petals of the apple-blossom's youth when the labourious time comes for his work in the world and for the bearing of apples. And I am robed each day and every night anew with the beauty of heaven, and I make lovely visions of the trees. But Man! What is Man? In the ancient parliament of the elder hills, when the grey ones speak together, they say nought of Man, but concern themselves only with their brethren the stars. Or when they wrap themselves in purple cloaks at evening, they lament some old irreparable wrong, or, uttering some mountain hymn, all mourn the set of sun."

"Your beauty," said the road, "and the beauty of the sky, and of the rhododendron blossom and of spring, live only in the mind of Man, and except in the mind of Man the mountains have no voices. Nothing is beautiful that has not been seen by Man's eye. Or if your rhododendron blossom was beautiful for a moment, it soon withered and was drowned, and spring soon passes away; beauty can only live on in the mind of Man. I bring thought into the mind of Man swiftly from distant places every day. I know the Telegraph—I know him well; he and I have walked for hundreds of miles together. There is no work in the world except for Man and the making of his cities. I take wares to and fro from city to city."

"My little stream in the field there," said the river, "used to make wares in that house for awhile once."

"Ah," said the road, "I remember, but I brought cheaper ones from distant cities. Nothing is of any importance but making cities for Man."

"I know so little about him," said the river, "but I have a great deal of work to do—I have all this water to send down to the sea; and then to-morrow or next day all the leaves of Autumn will be coming this way. It will be very beautiful. The sea is a very, very wonderful place. I know all about it; I have heard shepherd boys singing of it, and sometimes before a storm the gulls come up. It is a place all blue and shining and full of pearls, and has in it coral islands and isles of spice, and storms and galleons and the bones of Drake. The sea is much greater than Man. When I come to the sea, he will know that I have worked well for him. But I must hurry, for I have much to do. This bridge delays me a little; some day I will carry it away."

"Oh, you must not do that," said the road.

"Oh, not for a long time," said the river. "Some centuries perhaps—and I have much to do besides. There is my song to sing, for instance, and that alone is more beautiful than any noise that Man makes."

"All work is for Man," said the road, "and for the building of cities. There is no beauty or romance or mystery in the sea except for the men that sail abroad upon it, and for those that stay at home and dream of them. As for your song, it rings night and morning, year in, year out, in the ears of men that are born in Wrellisford; at night it is part of their dreams, at morning it is the voice of day, and so it becomes part of their souls. But the song is not beautiful in itself. I take these men with your song in their souls up over the edge of the valley and a long way off beyond, and I am a strong and dusty road up there, and they go with your song in their souls and turn it into music and gladden cities. But nothing is the Work of the World except work for Man."

"I wish I was quite sure about the Work of the World," said the stream; "I wish I knew for certain for whom we work. I feel almost sure that it is for the sea. He is very great and beautiful. I think that there can be no greater master than the sea. I think that some day he may be so full of romance and mystery and sound of sheep bells and murmur of mist-hidden hills, which we streams shall have brought him, that there will be no more music or beauty left in the world, and all the world will end; and perhaps the

streams shall gather at the last, we all together, to the sea.
Or perhaps the sea will give us at the last unto each one his
own again, giving back all that he has garnered in the years
—the little petals of the apple-blossom and the mourned ones
of the rhododendron, and our old visions of the trees and
sky; so many memories have left the hills. But who may
say? For who knows the tides of the sea?"

"Be sure that it is all for Man," said the road. "For Man
and the making of cities."

Something had come near on utterly silent feet.

"Peace, peace!" it said "You disturb the queenly night,
who, having come into this valley, is a guest in my dark
halls. Let us have an end to this discussion."

It was the spider who spoke.

"The Work of the World is the making of cities and
palaces. But it is not for Man. What is Man? He only
prepares my cities for me, and mellows them. All his works
are ugly, his richest tapestries are coarse and clumsy. He
is a noisy idler. He only protects me from mine enemy the
wind; and the beautiful work in my cities, the curving out-
lines and the delicate weavings, is all mine. Ten years to a
hundred it takes to build a city, for five or six hundred more
it mellows, and is prepared for me; then I inhabit it, and
hide away all that is ugly, and draw beautiful lines about it
to and fro. There is nothing so beautiful as cities and palaces; they are the loveliest places in the world, because they
are the stillest, and so most like the stars. They are noisy
at first, for a little, before I come to them; they have ugly
corners not yet rounded off, and coarse tapestries, and then
they become ready for me and my exquisite work, and are
quite silent and beautiful. And there I entertain the regal
nights when they come there jewelled with stars, and all
their train of silence, and regale them with costly dust. Already nods, in a city that I wot of, a lonely sentinel whose
lords are dead, who grows too old and sleepy to drive away
the gathering silence that infests the streets; to-morrow I

go to see if he be still at his post. For me Babylon was built, and rocky Tyre; and still men build my cities! All the Work of the World is the making of cities, and all of them I inherit."

THE DOOM OF LA TRAVIATA

EVENING stole up out of mysterious lands and came down on the streets of Paris, and the things of the day withdrew themselves and hid away, and the beautiful city was strangely altered, and with it the hearts of men. And with lights and music, and in silence and in the dark, the other life arose, the life that knows the night, and dark cats crept from the houses and moved to silent places, and dim streets became haunted with dusk shapes. At this hour in a mean house, near to the Moulin Rouge, La Traviata died; and her death was brought to her by her own sins, and not by the years of God. But the soul of La Traviata drifted blindly about the streets where she had sinned till it struck against the wall of Notre Dame de Paris. Thence it rushed upwards, as the sea mist when it beats against a cliff, and streamed away to Paradise, and was there judged. And it seemed to me, as I watched from my place of dreaming, when La Traviata came and stood before the sea of judgment, that clouds came rushing up from the far Paradisal hills and gathered together over the head of God, and became one black cloud; and the clouds moved swiftly as shadows of the night when a lantern is swung in the hand, and more and more clouds rushed up, and ever more and more, and, as they gathered, the cloud a little above the head of God became no larger, but only grew blacker and blacker. And the halos of the saints settled lower upon their heads and narrowed and became pale, and the singing of the choirs of the seraphim faltered and sunk low, and the converse of the blessed suddenly ceased. Then a stern look came into the face of God, so that the seraphim turned away and left Him, and the saints. Then God commanded, and seven great angels rose up slowly through the clouds that carpet Paradise, and there was pity on their faces, and their eyes were closed. Then God pronounced judgment, and the lights of Paradise went out, and the azure crystal windows that look towards the world, and the windows rouge and verd, became dark and colourless, and I saw no more. Presently the seven great angels came out by one of Heaven's gates and set their faces Hellwards, and four of them carried the young soul of La Traviata, and one of them went on before and one of them followed behind. These six trod with mighty strides the long and dusty road that is named the Way of the Damned. But the seventh flew above them all the way, and the light of the fires of Hell that was hidden from the six by the dust of that dreadful road flared on the feathers of his breast.

Presently the seven angels, as they swept Hellwards, uttered speech.

"She is very young," they said; and "She is very beautiful," they said; and they looked long at the soul of La Traviata, looking not at the stains of sin, but at that portion of her soul wherewith she had loved her sister a long while dead, who flitted now about an orchard on one of Heaven's hills with a low sunlight ever on her face, who communed daily with the saints when they passed that way going to bless the dead from Heaven's utmost edge. And as they looked long at the beauty of all that remained beautiful in her soul they said: "It is but a young soul;" and they would have taken her to one of Heaven's hills, and would there have given her a cymbal and a dulcimer, but they knew that the Paradisal gates were clamped and barred against La Traviata. And they would have taken her to a valley in the world where there were a great many flowers and a loud sound of streams, where birds were singing always and church bells rang on Sabbaths, only this they durst not do. So they swept onward nearer and nearer Hell. But when they were come quite close and the glare was on their faces, and they saw the gates already divide and prepare to open outwards, they said: "Hell is a terrible city, and she is tired of cities;" then suddenly they dropped her by the side of the road, and wheeled and flew away. But into a great pink flower that was horrible and lovely grew the soul of La Traviata; and it had in it two eyes but no eyelids, and it stared constantly into the faces of all the passers-by that went along the dusty road to Hell; and the flower grew in the glare of the lights of Hell, and withered but could not die; only, one petal turned back towards the heavenly hills as an ivy leaf turns outwards to the day, and in the soft and silvery light of Paradise it withered not nor faded, but heard at times the commune of the saints coming murmuring from the distance, and sometimes caught the scent of orchards wafted from the heavenly hills, and felt a faint breeze cool it every evening at the hour when the saints to Heaven's edge went forth to bless the dead.

But the Lord arose with His sword, and scattered His disobedient angels as a thresher scatters chaff.

ON THE DRY LAND

OVER the marshes hung the gorgeous night with all his wandering bands of nomad stars, and his whole host of still ones blinked and watched.

Over the safe dry land to eastward, grey and cold, the first clear pallor of dawn was coming up above the heads of the immortal gods.

Then, as they neared at last the safety of the dry land, Love looked at the man whom he had led for so long through the marshes, and saw that his hair was white, for it was shining in the pallor of the dawn.

Then they stepped together on to the land, and the old man sat down weary on the grass, for they had wandered in the marshes for many years; and the light of the grey dawn widened above the heads of the gods.

And Love said to the old man, "I will leave you now."

And the old man made no answer, but wept softly.

Then Love was grieved in his little careless heart, and he said: "You must not be sorry that I go, nor yet regret me, nor care for me at all.

"I am a very foolish child, and was never kind to you, nor friendly. I never cared for your great thoughts, or for what was good in you, but perplexed you by leading you up and down the perilous marshes. And I was so heartless that, had you perished where I led you, it would have been nought to me, and I only stayed with you because you were good to play with.

"And I am cruel and altogether worthless and not such a one as any should be sorry for when I go, or one to be regretted, or even cared for at all."

And still the old man spoke not, but wept softly; and Love grieved bitterly in his kindly heart.

And Love said: "Because I am so small my strength has been concealed from you, and the evil that I have done. But my strength is great, and I have used it unjustly. Often I pushed you from the causeway through the marshes, and cared not if you drowned. Often I mocked you, and caused others to mock you. And often I led you among those that hated me, and laughed when they revenged themselves upon you.

"So weep not, for there is no kindness in my heart, but only murder and foolishness, and I am no companion for one so wise as you, but am so frivolous and silly that I laughed when they revenged themselves upon you.

"So weep not, for there is no kindness in my heart, but only murder and foolishness, and I am no companion for one so wise as you, but am so frivolous and silly that I laughed at your noble dreams and hindered all your deeds. See now, you have found me out, and now you will send me away, and here you will live at ease, and, undisturbed, have noble dreams of the immortal gods.

"See now, here is dawn and safety, and *there* is darkness and peril."

Still the old man wept softly.

Then Love said: "Is it thus with you?" and his voice was grave now and quiet. "Are you so troubled? Old friend of so many years, there is grief in my heart for you. Old friend of perilous ventures, I must leave you now. But I will send my brother soon to you—my little brother Death. And he will come up out of the marshes to you, and will not forsake you, but will be true to you as I have not been true."

And dawn grew brighter over the immortal gods, and the

old man smiled through his tears, which glistened won-
drously in the increasing light. But Love went down to the
night and to the marshes, looking backward over his shoulder as he went, and smiling beautifully about his eyes. And
in the marshes whereunto he went, in the midst of the gorgeous night, and under the wandering bands of nomad stars,
rose shouts of laughter and the sounds of the dance.

And after a while, with his face towards the morning,
Death out of the marshes came up tall and beautiful, and
with a faint smile shadowy on his lips, and lifted in his arms
the lonely man, being gentle with him, and, murmuring with
his low deep voice an ancient song, carried him to the
morning, to the gods.

THE END